phantorama *n*. Very rare condition
which gives the ability to see ghosts.
Can be cool, but mostly just freaky…

fiona dunbar

ORCHARD

ORCHARD BOOKS
338 Euston Road, London NW1 3BH
Orchard Books Australia
Level 17/207 Kent Street, Sydney, NSW 2000

First published in the UK in 2011 by Orchard Books

ISBN 978 1 40830 929 2

A CIP catalogue record for this book is available from the British Library.

3 5 7 9 10 8 6 4 2

Printed in Great Britain

Orchard Books is a division of Hachette Children's Books,
an Hachette UK company.

www.hachette.co.uk

For George

Ten Days

I'm a WRECK.

Think I need to sleep for about a week – only right now I'm still buzzing from everything that's happened. Feels like someone filled up my veins with fizzling Coke.

We're out on the road again, heading to the west country...leaving Oxenden behind. I can't believe it's only TEN DAYS since we first arrived at that place! Ten days. Seems way longer – and I swear I feel more like ten YEARS older. So much has happened...

God, I've just looked back at my last blog entry before we went there! Blathering on about how weird it is having this phantorama thing, and no

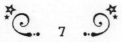

one understands what it's like, blah, blah...I hadn't experienced the half of it! OK, so seeing ghosts for the first time IS a big deal. But I had NO idea what I was in for...

Weird Atmosphere

Ten days earlier…

I sensed it the moment we walked into the house. What 'it' was exactly, I hadn't a clue, but the air crackled with…what? Tension? Menace? *Something.*

We were visiting friends who lived in Oxenden, this village by the Thames that's barely five centimetres out of London. Not exactly an epic journey. I was all psyched for getting way out there in our new life of travelling in our new camper van, the Hippo – to places like Cornwall and Scotland, like we'd planned… Instead, here we were, just off the M4, near Maidenhead. Bit like Scott of the Antarctic getting as far as Bognor Regis.

But driving a great big Hippo took some getting used to, Maro explained. 'Cornwall is a *long* drive to do straight off in a huge bus like this!' she said.

Well, what Maro says goes. And fair play to her,

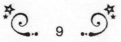

she's our gran and she's raising the three of us – me, my brother Sam, and my sister Flossie – single-handedly. Which now involves home-schooling, *plus* being the Hippo driver.

So Oxenden it was, and Dinky Vyner's house. Ha! Dinky. Hilarious name because to be honest, she's anything *but* dinky – what Maro would call 'big-boned'. And *way* younger than Maro, like a lot of her friends are. That's my grandma for you – young at heart. Anyway, Maro really wanted to visit Dinky and her family because we hadn't seen them for ages (a Good Thing as far as I was concerned, but that's another story). They'd known each other since before us lot were even born: back then, Maro was working in the Athena Restaurant, and Dinky was one of her favourite customers. There was always extra retsina and baklava for Dinky – no doubt a good part of why she's so non-dinky now. She's nice, in a rather OTT way: all bouncy and larger-than-life. Bit in your face at first, but you get used to it. Not someone you forget in a hurry. Maro really missed her when she moved out of town. All the same, Dinky was really supportive to Maro when our Mum died…no, don't feel sorry for me. I don't even remember her, I was so little. And Maro's as good as any mum.

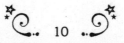

'Well, we may not have gone far distance-wise,' said Sam, gazing out the window, 'but look at this place; it's like we just travelled back in time about a hundred years.'

It was true – this was your classic sleepy village. All mossy, half-timbered houses about five centuries old. Main street basically consisting of a pub, a church and a shop. Population: about twenty-seven, by the look of it. Probably about as many ghosts as live inhabitants, I reckoned. The few people we saw certainly looked as if they were from another era.

When the Hippo lumbered into Dinky's driveway, there she was, bounding out of the house like an oversized puppy. She and Maro did that whole squeezing-the-life-out-of-each-other and making-excited-noises thing that only women over a certain age do. 'Mmmmmm! It's so lovely to seeeeee yoooooo!' *Squeeze, squeeze.* 'Ooh, and look at yooooo!' (to us). 'So gorgeous!' *Squish, squash.* Plus plenty of Gringlish from our Greek grandma, like you always get when she's either super-happy or off her head with fury.

For a moment, I thought I saw a flicker of something on Dinky's face – like a cloud passing in front of the sun. Then she was all bright again, saying, 'I love this Hippo thing. Isn't it great?'

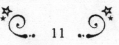

Dinky's husband appeared. He reached out and shook Maro's hand. 'Hello Maro, lovely to see you again.'

'Hello…hello!' said Maro.

I cringed, because she'd obviously forgotten his name, and was repeating the 'hello' to make up for it, like she always did in these situations. To be honest, I couldn't remember it either.

'You remember Charlie, don't you?' said Dinky, helpfully.

'….Charlie!' said Maro, like she'd meant all along to add the name onto the double hello. 'Charlie, Charlie,' she went on, clearly overcompensating at this point.

'Well, come on in,' said Charlie. 'Let me take your bags.'

We crunched up the gravel drive and went into the house.

And that's when it hit me.

Something was definitely up here; I could *taste* it. I glanced around: comfy place, low ceilings, lots of antiques, smell of fresh paint. They'd only recently moved in. No ghosts, though – not that I could see. Which didn't mean there weren't any, of course…

'Louis? Emily?' yelled Dinky. 'Oh, where are those kids?'

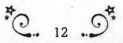

It was years since we'd last seen Louis and Emily. Back then, Sam had latched onto Louis, the Big Boy, like some pathetic faithful puppy. And the two little girls, Floss and Em, had been like Siamese twins. Ick…

'I told them to be back by five,' said Dinky. 'So rude of them, I am sorry–'

'Don't worry!' said Maro.

No, really, don't, I thought. I was in no big fat hurry to see either of them, frankly – especially Louis.

'Honestly, that boy!' said Dinky. 'He's *obsessed* with going out in that boat, heaven knows where he gets to.'

Maro looked alarmed. 'A boat? Oh, I hope he's OK…'

'Oh, he'll be fine,' said Dinky. 'It's just a little rowing boat, and he's an excellent rower–'

'Excellent swimmers, too, both of 'em!' laughed Charlie. 'Never mind, come upstairs, and I'll show you where you're sleeping.'

We followed him upstairs, and the atmosphere seemed to calm down a bit. I wondered why.

'Sam, we've put you in with Louis, and all the girls together, OK?' said Charlie.

Can't wait, I thought. Here I was, odd one out again. Louis-and-Sam, Floss-and-Em…and Kitty. *Oh joy.*

'Is it me, or is there a weird atmosphere in this

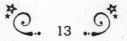

house?' I asked Flossie, after Charlie had left us to unpack our things and settle in.

'What do you mean, like a bad smell or something?'

'No, I mean…god, I don't know how to describe it…it's a bad feeling. A sort of tension. Like…' I trailed off. What I was *going* to say was, it was almost as if there was something lurking in the walls – but I didn't want to freak Flossie out. 'Oh, I dunno, maybe I'm imagining it.'

'Well, everything seems normal to me,' said Flossie. 'So maybe you are. Unless it's a ghost?'

'Hmm…well, it's not like I've actually *seen* anything.'

'Maybe you've just got a duff feeling about the place 'cause you basically don't want to be here,' said Flossie.

I flopped down on Emily's bed, with its sickly-sweet girly flower-patterned duvet cover. 'Yeah, well…'

Sam appeared in the doorway. 'Getting impatient, Kitty?' he said, with a mischievous grin. 'Can't wait to see your *bezzy mate* Louis?'

I gave him a withering look. 'Yeah, right. As if.'

'Well, I can't wait to see Emily,' said Flossie. 'I hope they hurry up.'

'How d'you even remember her, Floss?' said Sam. 'It's been like, four years. You were barely out of nappies!'

'I was six!' said Flossie. 'And I do *so* remember her.'

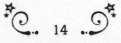

14

Sam plonked himself on the bed next to me and jabbed me in the ribs. 'Here, what about that time in the woods, with the sw–'

'Shut up, Sam,' I said, nudging him – well, punching him – back.

'Ha ha ha ha....ow!' Sam laughed and winced at the same time.

'The what?' asked Flossie.

The swing, he was going to say. It was not an incident I wanted to remember.

'You know it was completely unfair, what Louis did,' I said.

'*What* did he do?' Flossie persisted.

I sighed. 'He hung a rope swing from a tree in the woods, for getting across this stream, OK? And he dared me to go first, but it was completely unfair, because–'

'She fell in,' said Sam.

'The rope was too short! I swear he did it on purpose.'

Sam was still sniggering. 'It *was* funny, though.'

'Yeah well, frankly, *Sam*, all Louis had to do was sneeze, and you'd be all, "oh, Louis, that's the best sneeze ever, how d'you *do* that?"'

'What the hell are you talking about?'

'You know exactly what I'm talking about,' I said.

 15

'Following him around like a faithful puppy all the time…it was pretty vomit-inducing.'

'Oh yawn, Kitty, get over yourself,' said Sam. 'You just couldn't *deal* with him, that was your problem.'

I ignored him. 'Just don't be like it this time,' I said. 'You're older now, have a little self-respect.'

Sam groaned loudly.

'Well, Louis is older too,' said Flossie, gazing out of the window. 'Maybe he's changed. Maybe he's nicer now…oh hey, they've got a trampoline. Let's go outside!'

We headed downstairs, and *whoosh*, the weird feeling came swooping up at me again. We went past the kitchen, where Dinky was clattering around, muttering, 'Where *did* I put that corkscrew?' Then we were outside…and the feeling lifted again.

Sam started kicking a football around, and Flossie went for a bounce on the trampoline. I stood for a moment, gazing back at the house. *Was* the weird feeling really just me not wanting to be here? No – it would hardly be limited to indoors, on the ground floor, if that was the case. This was definitely something stronger than that. *Sickly, bitter.* And yet…still no sign of any ghosts. Strange.

I turned and wandered to the end of the garden, past

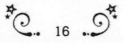

16

flowerbeds and a couple of sheds, into a tangle of overgrown shrubbery. A flicker of white caught my eye. Thinking it might be a ghost, I pushed the shrubs out of the way, then saw that I'd reached water, and the white thing was a swan.

'Hey guys, check this out!' I called. 'It's the river.'

Sam and Floss came over. 'That's not the Thames,' said Sam. 'It's too narrow.'

'Oh yeah, I guess,' I said, gazing at the weeping willows trailing in the black water just a couple of metres away.

A moment later, a small wooden boat appeared. Standing up in it, pushing it along with a punt, was a tall, thin boy. Baggy sweatshirt with rolled-up sleeves, tousled mop of brown hair. I could tell right away it was Louis. He had pale eyes set really far apart, like an alien or something. Sitting in the boat was a girl, Emily. Same alien eyes, but lighter hair. A golden retriever stood beside them – I realised it had to be the same dog they'd had all those years ago, only now she was fat as a barrel, her coat faded and dull.

'Hey, you're here,' said Louis coolly, as he leaped onto the bank and tied the boat to its post. He helped Emily out, while the dog clambered out clumsily, getting wet. She shook herself, spraying water all over us.

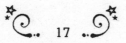

'Hetty!' cried Emily. 'You silly girl!' She turned to Flossie. 'Sorry!'

'It's OK,' said Flossie.

They gazed at each other shyly. Four years – practically half a lifetime for them. I could see they were sussing each other out all over again.

I couldn't think of anything to say either, other than 'Hi'. There was an awkward silence. Finally Sam said, 'That's the same dog you had before, right?' Talk about lame.

'Yeah,' said Louis. 'She's getting kind of old now. Anyway, I'm starving. C'mon.'

We headed indoors.

Dinky, Charlie and Maro were in the kitchen, getting dinner ready. 'Well, have you checked the dishwasher?' Charlie was saying as we came in.

'Of course I have...oh, *there* you are!' said Dinky, peering out from behind a cupboard door. 'Louis, have you seen the colander anywhere?'

'The what?'

'The colander. I can't find it.'

'Oh!' Louis clicked his fingers. 'Sorry! I left it in the garden. I was playing at soldiers.'

'Oh, for heaven's sake–'

'Kidding!' said Louis. 'Mum, *really*.' He turned to us.

'Don't mind Mum, she's been a bit forgetful lately.' He patted Dinky on the shoulder. 'It'll turn up.'

'Yes, but I want it now!'

'Em, check the bathroom cabinet,' said Louis. He turned to us again. 'You think I'm joking, but the other day, I couldn't find my football boots. Eventually found them in the washing machine.'

'Ah well, moving house, you know,' said Charlie. 'Always chaos!'

'Charlie, it's been a whole *month*,' said Dinky.

Maro had been peering into cupboards all this time, and finally held up a large sieve. 'What about this?'

'Oh, that'll do,' said Dinky. 'Thanks, Maro…oh, what are we like, eh? Pour us some more wine, will you, love? Come on, let's eat!'

The kitchen was too small for all of us, so we ate in the dining room. It was a bit posh: all antique furniture, loads of pictures, deep blood-red walls…some old dude in a white wig staring down at us from over the fireplace.

I gazed at the plateful of stew I'd been handed, and realised I had absolutely zero appetite. I forced myself to eat a couple of mouthfuls, and it was nice, but I just wasn't hungry. The bad atmosphere seemed to have turned my stomach. I found my eye wandering to the portrait on the wall.

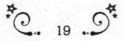

'Do you like it?' said Dinky.

'Oh yes, really tasty, thanks,' I said, picking up an extra-large forkful of stew. 'Mmm!'

Dinky smiled. 'Oh good – but I actually meant the painting.'

'Oh! Er…mm-hmm,' I nodded, mouth full of stew.

'It's our ancestor,' said Louis. 'Cool wig, huh? I want one.'

Sam snickered.

Here we go, I thought, *the Louis fan club all over again.*

'*My* ancestor, to be precise,' said Dinky. 'Sir Ambrose Vyner.'

'Ah yes, I remember you telling me about him once,' said Maro. 'Funny though, I don't remember the portrait at all.'

'No, we only got it recently,' said Dinky. Then she and Charlie went into some lengthy description of how they'd been trying to track it down for years, blah blah…I kind of tuned out.

But I was curious about the portrait. Could that be where the strange atmosphere was coming from? I remembered the ghosts in the antique shop we lived above in London – they each had a piece of furniture they'd become eternally attached to. When the piece was sold, the ghost went along with it. Could the

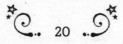

painting be haunted? Maybe by Sir Ambrose himself? It would explain why I only had the strange feeling downstairs. Whatever it was, I seemed to be the only one who sensed it – so it had to be ghost-related.

The question was: *who was the ghost, and what were they up to?*

Smashing Time

'Can I have some more of those?' I asked.

'Sure, help yourself,' said Emily, passing over the tub of chocolate Rice Krispie bites. Now that I was upstairs, away from the weird atmosphere, I was famished.

'Thanks,' I said, stuffing my face. At Dinky's insistence, the five of us had played a game of Cluedo together – some bogus adult idea of a 'bonding' thing. After that, Sam went off with Louis into his room, and Floss and Em soon descended into Girly Giggledom, having been all shy around each other to start with. Yup – things were panning out *exactly* as they had last time around.

I got into bed, plugged myself into my iPod to tune them out, and started some serious online chat on my laptop. I must have zizzed off, 'cause the next thing I knew I was woken by a sudden noise – a sort of tinkling

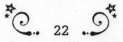

sound. My earphones had fallen out, and everything else was dead quiet. No traffic, nothing – silent as the grave. It was a bit creepy – I was used to the comforting round-the-clock hum of London. Here, there was nothing. But I'd definitely heard *something*. I checked the time on my phone: 2.47am.

I lay there for a bit, just staring into the darkness above me, the way you do when you're listening out for something in the night. Why do we do that? As if *staring* will somehow make you hear better…

Then there was another little tinkle-smash sound…then another.

Floss and Em just slept on.

Should I go downstairs to investigate? But what if it was an intruder? No, it couldn't be, I decided. Hetty would be going mental by now if it was. She'd probably just knocked something over by accident herself. But then…this didn't sound like an accident. It had been a whole series of little smashes. Like it was deliberate.

Then again: *tinkle-smash*.

OK. I would have to go down and check it out. *Courage, girl, courage*, I told myself. *How bad can it be?* I got up and crept downstairs to the kitchen. It was gloomy down there, but between the cold blue light of the moon and the warm orangey light coming from the

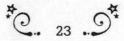

hallway, I could pretty much make stuff out. Enough to see the mess on the floor, glinting shards of glass…

Out of the corner of my eye I saw something whoosh by, then *smash!* Another glass on the floor. I turned to where it had come from, and there was another, flying off the shelf…then another.

There was *nobody* there – the glasses were flying off the shelf all by themselves. And the shelf was perfectly level.

What the hell was going on?

I thought I heard Hetty whining – yes, I could see the shape of her, a dark shadow, moving in the hallway. Poor Hetty, she was terrified. Too scared to bark.

Another glass. *Smash!* And another one.

Then I caught a glimpse of white bathrobe moving down the stairs. For some reason – perhaps because I thought I might be seen as the culprit – I didn't want anyone to know I was down here, so I hid behind the door. The kitchen light went on, and I heard Dinky's voice: 'Oh, Hetty, there, there!'

Hetty clearly didn't know whether to bark or whimper, so just sort of did both, while Dinky went on trying to soothe her. A muffled voice came from somewhere else in the house – Emily? – and Dinky said, 'It's nothing, darling. Just a…a shelf that's come down. Go back to bed, sweetie.'

A shelf that's come down? I could see for myself that wasn't what happened. Dinky was lying. I guessed she didn't want to freak Emily out.

There followed an awkward few minutes while Dinky got a dustpan and brush and swept up the glass. Then the light went off, and I was alone again.

GHOST BLOG

FRIDAY 1 APRIL 3.14AM

OK, so there's definitely SOMETHING ghosty going on in Dinky's house. But why can't I SEE it?

Maybe it's a poltergeist? Poltergeists move things around, don't they? Maybe this one moved the corkscrew, the colander and Louis' football boots, as well as smashing the glasses. Here's the thing: in stories, people see ghosts (even people without phantorama – yeah, right!) but they never see poltergeists.

But I DO have phantorama! And even I don't see this one.

OK, but am now remembering that I've already witnessed a poltergeist in action. I watched him write on

a whiteboard with a marker pen…and WHEN HE DID THAT, HE WAS INVISIBLE. Even to me. Unlike all the other times, when he wasn't moving stuff, and I could see him only too well. It's like the spirits have limited energy and it's used up in one thing or the other.

So let's suppose it is a poltergeist. The next things to figure out are:

1. Who is it? IS it the old ancestor from the portrait?
2. Whoever it is, WHY are they doing this? And how do I find out?
3. If this happens again, maybe I can get them to stop smashing things or whatever, and appear to me – and TALK to me.
4. FIND OUT MORE ABOUT THE ANCESTOR GUY!

'Look at this shoddy workmanship!' complained Charlie, next morning. He was up a ladder in the kitchen, fixing the shelf that had supposedly 'fallen down' during the night.

He sighed loudly. 'And not cheap, I might add! I don't know why I bother getting people in to do these jobs. Better off doing them myself.' He sighed again while he drilled away at the bracket.

Well, clearly he was in on this whole ruse too – unless Dinky had actually taken the shelf down, which would be a bit extreme. I felt sure she'd told him what had really happened, and he was putting on this act for our benefit. All that sighing was a bit OTT; he wasn't a very convincing actor.

Dinky appeared in the doorway, looking washed out. 'Can you believe it, a shelf just collapsing like that?' She pointed to a black rubbish bag nearby. 'Thirteen broken glasses!'

'You should get whoever put the shelf up to pay for those,' said Maro.

'Er…yes, right, I should!' said Dinky. 'Well, well…breakfast…'

'Don't you worry, *agapi-mou*, I'll take care of it,' said Maro. 'You go on, I know you have to get to work.'

'Yes, well…I'm so sorry we couldn't get any time off while you're here. But since we're going to France next week…'

'Of course,' said Maro. 'It's OK, really.'

'Well…here are mugs,' said Dinky brightly. 'You'll have to use these for your juice.'

The shadow was gone from her face and she was back to the usual big, jolly Dinky – but I could tell how stressed out she was. She was like one of those screens

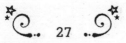

27

they sometimes put up in front of buildings when they're being renovated, where they put a picture of the building on it. You can see all the windows and stuff, just as it should be – only it's a façade. Behind it is a bit of a wreck.

'OK, well...eggs,' said Dinky, opening the fridge door. 'We have eg...aah!'

Maro, Charlie and I peered inside. There, on the floor of the fridge, was a whole swimming mass of smashed eggs. Hetty nosed her way through and began lapping them up.

'No, Hetty!' said Dinky, pulling her back. 'Honestly, I have no idea how–'

'Oh, these things happen,' said Maro, clearly just trying to make her feel better about all the weirdness. 'Don't you worry about it, we'll be fine. Go! Get to work. I'll sort all this out.'

Dinky sighed. 'Bless you, Maro...OK, I'm gone. And you just...take it easy. Let the kids do their own thing. Louis'll be in charge, won't you, Louis?'

'Yeah,' said Louis.

Oh, I bet you will, I thought.

The Island Boys

Smashed glasses, smashed eggs…what next? No way did those eggs smash themselves, any more than the glasses did.

I was curious to see how Emily behaved after her night-time disturbance, but I guessed she'd forgotten about it as she didn't seem troubled at all. She and Flossie were giggling away, same as ever.

I managed to snatch a moment with Sam while we were putting our shoes on by the back door.

'So how was your night?' I asked. 'Sleep well?' There wasn't much else I could say, not with the girls right there.

'Yeah, fine.'

'So…that shelf that collapsed in the night. You didn't hear anything?'

'Oh, that. No.'

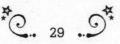

'Oh. Still, I guess Louis' room is off down the other end of the house, isn't it?'

'Uh-huh.' Sam glanced up from tying his shoelaces. 'Kit? Is something bothering you?'

'Me? Oh, no. No, no, no.' I was overcompensating, just like Maro. 'I'm cool.'

Sam was still looking at me. 'Uh-huh. OK, well…good.'

It was the first day of half term for Louis and Emily, and Louis, surprise surprise, wanted to take us out in his boat. Somehow, the five of us plus Hetty all managed to cram ourselves into it. I felt like a ten-ton weight, making the thing dip way down in the water as I stepped in, like it was going to sink any minute. Boats: I remembered now, I wasn't keen on boats.

Wasn't keen on the outing, full stop, to be honest. But since the other options consisted of hanging out at the house with the poltergeist, or going shopping with Maro for new glasses and eggs and stuff – well, it was a bit of a no-brainer.

Besides, maybe I could find out more from the others about the old ancestor, Sir Ambrose. If he was the poltergeist, what was his unfinished business? Because *all* ghosts had unfinished business, as far as I knew. It was their whole reason for haunting the

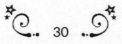

mortal world. So maybe Louis could give me some clues. I had to be careful, though. I had no idea how much he knew about the weirdness back at the house.

'So where are we going?' asked Sam, as Louis pushed us away from the bank with his punt.

'Depends,' said Louis. 'Can you keep a secret?'

'Oh, yeah, sure,' said Sam.

Louis looked at me and Floss.

'Cross my heart and hope to die,' said Flossie solemnly.

I shrugged. 'Yeah, whatever.' *Like I* care, *Louis*, I thought.

'Good. In that case, we'll go to my island.'

Flossie's mouth dropped open. 'You *own* an island?'

Louis smirked. 'No, of course I don't *own* it. But nobody else goes there. It's near a bunch of other better islands where people go for picnics and stuff. They don't bother with this one 'cause it's too small and there's no bridge. So we have it all to ourselves.'

'Who's "we"?' I asked.

'Louis has a gang that do *boy* stuff,' said Emily, rolling her eyes.

Oh great, I thought. Bunch of boys doing macho stuff, pretending they live in the wild. Shoot me now.

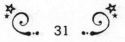

At best, this could be mind-crunchingly boring – at worst, I might be in for another round of humiliation. Had Louis changed in the *slightest* since the swing incident? Probably not. Probably couldn't wait for more fun and games at my expense...

'What do *you* do there, then?' Flossie asked Emily.

'Oh, me and my friends play house,' said Emily, cheerfully. 'It'll be fun with you! And you, of course,' she added, looking at me.

Gee, thanks, I thought. *Can't wait.*

The stream had joined the river, and the water was deeper now. Louis switched from punting to rowing.

'Louis,' I said.

'Yeah?'

'You know that ancestor of yours, Sir Ambrose?' I said. 'Do you know much about him?'

'Oh yeah, he was quite an important guy – he was in the government, and everything.'

'Really?'

'Uh-huh. But the best thing about him was, he was a member of the Hellfire Club.'

'The...the Hellfire Club?' I cleared my throat. 'Really? What was that?'

'Well, it was a secret club of really powerful people–'

'Devil-worshippers,' said Emily.

'Not *devil-worshippers*, Em,' said Louis. 'Well, not really…'

'What do you mean, not really?' I asked.

'Look, Sir Ambrose was a highly respected man – they all were. And the whole point of the club was, it was secret. Just like mine is. Hey, Sam, want a go?' he said, offering him the oars.

'Oh yeah, OK,' said Sam.

Hmm. *Change the subject, why don't you.*

My big question was dangling there, waiting to be asked: *how did he die?* But I couldn't figure out how to get it in without seeming weird. And anyway, Louis was busy instructing Sam on rowing technique. Then Sam wanted to know more about Louis' club, and I got roped into a discussion with the girls about secret hideaways I used to have when I was little. The moment had passed. Damn.

At no point in the journey did it occur to Louis to offer *me* the oars, I noticed. Typical. Although to be honest, I was pretty relieved. I'd probably have got us going round in circles and that would just give him another thing to be superior about.

We passed by the other islands, the popular ones. People were milling back and forth across a footbridge, and there were a few boats bobbing

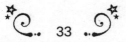

around too. Oxenden was getting into weekend mode. Eventually we came to a tiny island some way away from the rest of them. It was covered in trees, with no moorings or anything. Louis leaped onto the bank and secured the boat by tying the rope to a low branch. He helped Flossie and Emily out, then offered me a helping hand too. Ha! No thanks. The jury was still out on whether he was any less obnoxious than before. I didn't trust him not to play some practical joke on me.

'I can manage,' I said, and tried to do the leaping-elegantly-onto-the-bank thing he'd just done, but it all went wrong. The boat wobbled like crazy and I got into a bit of a panic. I went for it, but as I jumped I scraped my shin on the edge of the boat and landed on all fours in the mud. Yup – *really elegant.*

'Hey, you OK?' asked Louis.

'Yeah, 'mfine,' I said, picking myself up and wiping myself down as casually as I could. The scrape on my leg hurt like hell, but I just walked on, ignoring it.

'Ya-a-a-ay!' yelled Emily as she landed on the bank. Hetty got all het up, and they went hurtling off with Flossie to play house. I hesitated.

'You coming, then?' said Louis.

'Um…'

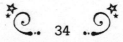

'Yeah, come on, Kit,' said Sam. 'You don't want to play *house*, for god's sake.'

'Cool,' said Louis. 'This way.'

Following him and Sam past Emily's 'house' of twigs and branches, I took the opportunity to check myself for mud and blood, and clean up as best I could. My top and shorts were OK, but I had a ladder in my tights – though at least the scrape on my shin wasn't bleeding.

When we got to the other side of the island, there were two other boys sitting on the bank, fishing. 'Hey,' said Louis, and introduced us to his friends, Jonah and Josh. Oh wow. Typical posh home-counties boys dressed in Hollister and Jack Wills. They annoyed me already.

I gazed back to where the girls were. Perhaps I should have hung out with them after all. Right, and play 'house', be the mummy or whatever. At least these guys were roughly my age. So what if they were all boys? Boys were people, weren't they? Even snooty public schoolboys. Plus it's not as if I'm super girly, or anything; I don't need to talk about make-up and fashion. *Deal with it, Kitty.*

But after about ten minutes of listening to the boys swap tips with Sam about fishing techniques, I was losing the will to live. Worse: next thing I knew, they

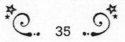 35

were talking about some sort initiation rites for their gang, the 'Insula Club'.

'Why d'you call it that?' asked Sam.

'It's Latin for "island",' said Louis.

Oh yeah, of course they had to have a *Latin* name.

'It's OK,' said Louis, grinning. 'There's no tarring and feathering, or anything. Just a couple of little tests. Technically, anyone who comes on the island has to join.' He looked at me.

A couple of little tests. Right. Just like that stupid rope swing.

'We don't want the *girl* though, Louis,' Jonah muttered.

Ha! I didn't know whether to be grateful to him for letting me off the hook, or annoyed at him for being so sexist.

'It's OK,' said Louis. 'We could bend the rules just this once.'

Like I *wanted* them to! 'I don't want to join, anyway,' I said quickly, stepping backwards.

'No, you should, Kit,' said Sam, tugging on my sleeve. 'She's cool,' he informed them, helpfully.

I yanked my sleeve away. 'No, you know what? I'm gonna go…check on the girls.'

Louis shrugged. 'If you want.'

'Yeah well, someone should be looking after them, y'know?'

Damn! How uncool did that sound?! Like such a nice, sensible girl. Which wasn't me at all. Embarrassed, I turned and walked away. Why didn't I just say exactly what I meant? That I didn't give a monkey's about their stupid gang. That, yes, I'd be perfectly able to pass their tests if I could be bothered. But I couldn't care less.

So now, any relief I felt at not having to swing through the trees like Tarzan or whatever, and make a complete idiot of myself, was cancelled out by the fact that they probably thought I was just a goody two-shoes. I stomped on through the crunchy leaves. 'Insula Club!' I found myself muttering. 'Just a couple of little tests…huh!'

Well, I'd show them. Didn't know *how*, but I would.

Fire

In the end, we didn't spend much longer on the island because the weather turned bad. By the afternoon it was pelting with rain, so we went to the movies. I had to wait till dinnertime to find out more about Sir Ambrose.

Once again, I had zero appetite. There was that weird, sickly feeling in the house that I still couldn't get used to. At least this time I'd had a big lunch, plus a whole bucket of popcorn and one of those massive supersize Cokes meant for people with bladders the size of elephants.

'Are you sure that's all you want?' said Dinky, after I'd accepted only a smidge of risotto.

'Yeah, I've got a bit of a...' I nearly said 'dodgy tummy', but then realised Louis might think it meant I had the squits. Hell, why did I *care* what he thought? Telling myself I didn't really want *anyone* thinking that,

I said, 'I'm just not that hungry right now, thanks. Maybe later.'

My eye wandered once again to the portrait of Sir Ambrose. He stared silently back at me in his haughty, rosy-cheeked, eighteenth-century way. I noticed he was posing with a white rose in his left hand. His fingers were kind of badly painted, actually – probably not a top artist. All the same, the painting had been stuck in this really OTT gilt frame, complete with a crest at the top with those stretched-out lions you see on flags and stuff, and some sort of motto at the bottom that I couldn't quite make out.

I still didn't know who or what was causing the weird atmosphere, or had smashed the glasses. I really needed more info about the house and its previous occupants. I reckoned Charlie was my best bet. After all, the house was his favourite subject.

Predictably, he was soon yammering on about the work they'd had done on it before they moved in. Meanwhile Floss and Em were asking me about my favourite bands, so I was kind of talking to them but at the same time eavesdropping on the adult conversation. When Charlie mentioned that something was 'just to be expected in a house this age', I spotted my chance and chipped in: 'Oh really? How old *is* it?'

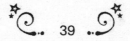

Sam gave me a funny look. It *was* a bit random of me, but hey.

'It's Georgian,' said Charlie, looking a bit surprised. 'Dates from 1790. What was interesting when we were having the renovation done, was just how much...' And he was off again, blathering on about the building work.

'Oh Charlie, really!' said Dinky, interrupting. 'Kitty doesn't want to hear all about sash windows and cornicing!' She turned to me. 'Why did you ask, Kitty?'

I shrugged. 'Oh, just wondered. *Ahem*, so it's like, not as old as the rest of the village, then? I thought Maro said the houses were mostly sort of Elizabethan or even Tudor...'

Dinky's face tensed up. 'Yes,' she said. 'There *was* an earlier house on this site, but–'

'...It got burned down,' added Emily. 'Sir Am–'

'Oh, Emily, I forgot to bring in the salad dressing,' Dinky said suddenly. 'Be a love and fetch it for me, will you?'

Emily frowned, but did as she was told and disappeared off into the kitchen. *Blatant* glances between Dinky and Charlie.

Dinky quickly changed the subject. 'So how was the movie?' she said, pouring herself another glass of wine (she'd had quite a bit already, I'd noticed). Good move on her part – the movie was either completely brilliant or utter rubbish, nobody could agree. So Floss, Sam and Louis launched into a heated discussion. The burned-down house was buried under a pile of amateur movie criticism.

My mind was churning. This *was* interesting. Clearly Dinky knew something about the fire that she didn't want to let on – something to do with Sir Ambrose. OK, now I was getting somewhere!

After dinner I joined in with Floss and Em's karaoke game. Not because I especially wanted to play, but just so I could ask Em more about the old house.

'It was an accident,' she explained, while she and I were meant to be listening to Flossie's rendition of, ironically, *I'm On Fire*. 'Sir Ambrose died in the fire.'

'So…he lived in the house that was here before this one?' I asked, as I stuffed my face with some cheese and crackers I'd brought upstairs.

'Yeah.'

'In this exact same spot?'

'Uh-huh. That's why Mum was so excited when the house came up for sale. "It's the next best thing to an ancestral home," she said. So even though it was falling to bits, she really wanted it. And Dad's just crazy about

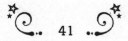

the garden. 'Specially those roses. Did you see the magic rosebush yet?'

'Magic rosebush?'

'Yeah. Flowers all year round, apparently, like magic. Dad thinks there's some kind of connection to the motto on the portrait.'

'What does it say?'

' "Oh plant again, eternal bloom". Weird, right? Cor, you really like cheese, don't you? You should be careful, might give you bad dreams.'

Ha! As if *bad dreams* were the problem. 'That's an old wives' tale,' I said.

'Why would old wives say that?'

'I dunno. Maybe they want to keep all the cheese for themselves,' I said, struggling to make myself heard over Flossie's warblings. 'So anyway – your mum. She doesn't like to talk about the fire, does she?'

Emily shrugged. 'I guess not. I don't know why it bothers her so much. It's not like she ever *knew* him or anything; he died two and a half centuries ago!'

'*I'm on fiiiire!*' sang Flossie. '*Wooh-oo-ooh!*'

'Well, sometimes the dead can have a hold over the living,' I said…which probably wasn't the most helpful thing to mention right at that moment, but it just sort of slipped out.

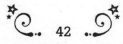

Emily looked alarmed.

'I mean…maybe she's just, like, really *interested* in him right now – since moving in here. And doesn't like to think of him getting…well, you know. Burned to death. That's all I meant. What happened – do you know?'

'Huh?'

'When the house burned down,' I said. 'Do you know what caused it?'

'Oh, I dunno…dropped lamp or something, I think.' Then Flossie finished her song, and Emily jumped up. 'OK, my go!'

So that was that – for now.

After a couple more rounds of karaoke I went to bed. I dropped off to sleep early – hardly surprising, what with the boredom factor, plus last night's disturbance. Next thing I knew, the room was dark, the girls were asleep, and I needed the loo. All that Coke was still working its way through me. I was really sleepy, though. Should I get up and deal with it, but risk being too wide-awake to get back to sleep? Or roll over and ignore the discomfort? I looked at the time: urgh. It was still only 12.30.

Then:

Tinkle-smash!

The poltergeist was back.

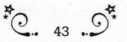

The Curse

OK, I had to get up now.

But heading across the landing to the bathroom, I got a shock – voices! People were talking downstairs. A split second later, I realised it was only Dinky and Maro. They were still up. And apparently the smashed glass was nothing to do with the poltergeist this time.

'No, no, don't worry about it, Dinky,' Maro was saying. 'Here, let me…'

Dinky didn't sound happy. 'No, I *do* worry about it! Look at this: how clumsy I am! Oh, it's all so…' She gave a huge sigh. 'This isn't how I wanted things to be. I'm not being any fun, and I…I *wanted* us to have fun.'

This kind of made me cringe, because there was a slight whininess in her voice that made her sound like an overgrown toddler complaining about not getting any sweets. She'd probably had too much wine.

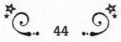

'Oh, don't talk such nonsense, Dinky,' Maro was saying. 'You're always fun!'

I should just leave them to it, I thought. Go to the loo and get back to bed. But then Dinky began to pour her heart out.

'It's the stress!' she cried. 'I just wish I wasn't so *stressed out*. I don't know…it's all this business with the house, and, you know…the *house*…'

I decided I should listen in on this. Ignoring my bladder, I crept downstairs. I sidled up alongside the kitchen door. Charlie had gone to bed, it seemed. Peering into the living room, I could just make out Hetty, sleeping beside the fading embers of the fire.

'But you've fixed the house,' Maro told Dinky. 'You're all settled in now!'

'You don't understand!' Dinky blurted out.

There was a pause.

'OK…' said Maro.

'There are forces at work that…Maro, you're going to think this is completely crazy…'

'No, no…go on.'

'I think this house is cursed,' announced Dinky.

You what? At first I didn't think I'd heard right.

'Oh, now come on–'

'Yes, that's what I'd have said, before,' said Dinky.

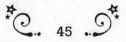 45

'I wouldn't have thought it possible. But…it goes back to Sir Ambrose's time. You see…the old house, the one that was here before this one? It burned down in 1769 – with Sir Ambrose in it. Maro, that was no accident.'

'Somebody deliberately started the fire?' said Maro.

'No, no…that's not what I mean,' said Dinky. I could hear the bottle clink against glass as she poured some more wine. 'There was a curse put on Sir Ambrose. The fire was just one of a series of things that happened to him.'

My eyes widened in the darkness as I huddled by the door.

'Oh, now, Dinky…' began Maro.

'No, listen to me!' said Dinky. 'You see, Sir Ambrose had this big falling out with another member of the Hellfire Club, John Wilkes. "That devil Wilkes", they called him. Ha! And not without reason! There was a massive rift in the Hellfire Club. The group fell apart when they disagreed over the war in Europe. That was the start of it – but the whole thing became more and more personal between Wilkes and Ambrose, denouncing each other publicly, that sort of thing. Wilkes couldn't *bear* the fact that Ambrose had so much influence over the Prime Minister. He did all he could to discredit him. Then, when that didn't work, he resorted to *black magic* –'

'But Dinky–' Maro tried to interrupt.

Dinky just carried right on. 'We know that Wilkes declared to friends that he would put a curse on Sir Ambrose. He said he'd take something belonging to him – you know, to direct the curse at him. We don't know what that thing was, but it would have been something small and portable – a watch, perhaps, or a snuffbox–'

'A what box?' said Maro.

'Snuff...you know, the powdered tobacco,' said Dinky. 'Oh, probably a very English thing, no one really uses it any more...'

'Not a Greek thing,' agreed Maro.

'Anyway, whatever it was, it was around this time that everything started to go wrong for Sir Ambrose. First his marriage broke down, then his health went into decline. He had a stroke and had to retire from politics. He went from being a lively, popular man to this grumpy, miserable old loner. He lost all his money and sold off a lot of possessions – including that portrait of him, of course – hence the fact that it still exists. Apparently he was the only one in the house when it burned down. He'd sacked the maid.'

'But Dinky,' Maro tried again.

'You can say that all those things might have

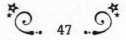

happened anyway,' said Dinky. 'You can say it's all superstitious nonsense, like I used to. We all did.'

'You've always known about this?' asked Maro.

'Oh, yes,' said Dinky. 'But it's not something we talk about much in my family. It's painful, you know? We prefer to remember Sir Ambrose for all the great things he did. So of course, it didn't put me off buying the place. But that was...before.'

'Before what?'

'Oh, Maro!' said Dinky, her voice raising an octave. I noticed Hetty stir in the living room.

'I think we've made a terrible mistake, moving in here! There *is* a malicious force at work, even now...even after one house was burned down, and another one built. The way things keep going missing...turning up in odd places...'

Hetty came padding over. I froze, trying to blend in with the wall and willing her not to make a fuss of me...

'...Oh, it all sounds so *minor* compared to what happened to Sir Ambrose,' Dinky was saying. 'But now things are getting worse. It's an evil spirit, so powerful it's lasted down the generations and couldn't even be purged by fire. It's still here, Maro. I'm sure of it now, after what happened last night with the glasses. And

somehow, it's growing in strength. I'm worried about what it's going to do next.'

Hetty made a soft little 'hello' sound, but thankfully Maro's voice drowned it out, as she asked about the people who'd lived there before. I quietly made my retreat back upstairs, worried that Hetty would give me away.

'Ha!' said Dinky. 'Yes, right, the people who lived here before, they didn't say anything, did they? Well, they wouldn't, would they? They wanted to get the hell out! They're hardly going to want to put a buyer off.'

'Well, no, but–'

'And now that I think of it, they did have a haunted look about them…hollow eyes– Hello?' The air crackled with tension. I froze, halfway up the stairs.

'Oh, thank god, it's only you, Hetty!' Dinky said. 'I thought it was…oh, Maro, this thing is making me so jumpy!'

GHOST BLOG

SATURDAY 2 APRIL 12.54AM

A curse!
  OMG this is *freaky stuff*.

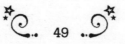

And it's completely turned all my thinking on its head. My haunted portrait theory is out, for starters. What if it isn't the ghost of Sir Ambrose himself that's causing trouble? What if it's all down to this curse? Only…what *is* a curse, exactly? Are ghosts involved? What did this Wilkes guy do, hire some kind of Rent-a-Poltergeist service, with no expiry date? Rent-a-Demon? And how can whatever he did still have power 250 years later? And after the fire, and everything. But that 'malicious force' is here all right, no question. I can feel it, taste it…I've SEEN the evidence.

Which must mean: there IS a ghostly element. Because I sense something here that others don't.

Oh no. Does that mean that IT senses ME as well? Is my presence making it all agitated? Because I'm thinking, the glasses smashing only just happened. Before that, for a whole month, it was just things going missing. Dinky herself said the 'evil spirit' was getting stronger.

Is it because of me?

Claustrophobia

The girls' babbling voices woke me next morning. Flossie was going on about something called the Hellfire Caves. I was still half asleep. The word 'Hellfire' struck a chord, and went hovering round in my brain, but I *so* didn't want to wake up, it was *way* too early...I pulled the duvet over my head.

Then all the stuff I'd overheard Dinky saying last night about the curse bubbled up in my brain, along with a horrible feeling of...guilt? Oh yeah. Because *I* was the problem, wasn't I? *I* was the one who was making things worse around here.

Maybe I'd have to sleep in the Hippo. I'd just make out I preferred to be alone. Ah, my brain was buzzing – no way was I getting back to sleep now. I flipped back the duvet.

'...Anyway, you're gonna love the caves,' Emily

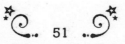

was saying. 'We've *got* to go there today...oh, hi Kitty.'

'Where's this?' I asked.

'The Hellfire Caves,' said Flossie, 'Oh, Kit, it sounds really cool! It's this long, winding Labrador–'

'*Labyrinth*,' corrected Emily.

'Yeah, labba...what she said, and it's the place where those eighteenth-century guys used to hang out – you know, the club their ancestor belonged to, the devil-worshippers? They held secret meetings there.'

I sat up. 'Seriously?'

'Yeah, it's famous for it,' said Emily. 'And it's haunted!'

'Oh?' I said, trying to seem nonchalant, and avoiding Flossie's knowing gaze. 'Who...who haunts them, then?'

'Oh, a bunch of people,' said Emily. 'There's this jilted bride, and a guy who had his heart ripped out–'

Louis and Sam appeared in the doorway. 'Lemme guess,' said Louis. 'You're talking about the Hellfire Caves.' He turned to Sam. 'They're really cheesy.'

Emily glared at him. 'They so *aren't* cheesy!' Turning back to Flossie, she gabbled on. 'Anyway, Mum said we were gonna do something all together today, and this is perfect. Wait till you see it – you go in and it's this tunnel, right, and it goes wa-a-ay down, deeper and

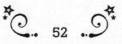

deeper, just keeps on going. And it gets *darker*, and *narrower*, and *colder*...'

'Yeah, and it's got all these stupid dummies in it, dressed up as Hellfire Club members,' interrupted Louis.

And ghosts, I thought. I really wanted to find out more about those. Maybe they would appear to me. Maybe, even, they would be able to give me some info about the curse... Oh yes, this would be very interesting!

One problem: Dinky. She was not keen *at all*.

'I'm sorry, Em, but there's been a change of plan,' she said over breakfast. 'We're going to go for a walk instead.'

'O-oh!' cried Emily. 'But we don't *want* to go for a walk. We want to go to the caves – don't we, Floss?'

Flossie stared at her Cheerios. 'Um...well...'

'I'm sorry,' said Dinky. 'It'll have to be some other time. We can go walking across the Chiltern Hills – it's a beautiful day out!'

Just then, we heard a rumble of thunder and the sky darkened ominously. Everyone stared at the window. In no time, big fat raindrops started hitting the windowpane.

Dinky stood there with her bowl of scrambled eggs. 'Ah. Well, there's always, um, the bowling alley...'

'Mum!' protested Emily. She turned to Charlie, who had just appeared with a pot of coffee. 'Dad!'

'Don't look at me,' said Charlie. 'I've got gardening to do – lots of pruning.'

'Da-ad!' Emily practically screamed.

'Oh, darling, you know Saturday is Daddy's gardening day,' said Dinky. 'Rain or shine.'

'And your mum was telling me she's worried about her claustrophobia,' added Maro.

'Claustrophobia?' said Louis. 'I never knew you–'

'Oh, I get it *terribly*,' insisted Dinky.

'She does…she does,' added Charlie.

'You just wouldn't know about it,' said Dinky, as she began dishing out scrambled eggs. 'We're never in such confined spaces…'

'But we've been to the caves together before!' protested Emily.

Dinky plonked down a plate of eggs with a thump. 'It comes and goes!' she snapped.

That shut everyone up for a bit.

'I know what,' said Emily. 'Maro could take us.'

'Well, I don't think–' Maro began.

'Oh, *please*?' said Emily. Really, the girl was shameless.

'Emily, Maro is your mother's friend,' said Charlie. 'They wanted to do something together today.'

Dinky stared at the rain, chewing her lip. 'On the

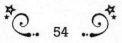

other hand… All right, look, I've got paperwork to catch up on anyway. If you don't mind, Maro…?'

'Oh, I don't mind at all,' said Maro. 'Is it far?'

'No, no – just at West Wycombe,' said Dinky. 'Thank you, Maro, we'll get together later. You'll only be gone for the morning. I'll give my cousin Carol a call – she works there. She'll get you a discount on tickets.'

So it was settled.

Meanwhile, the tension was getting so thick, you could slice it with a knife. At first I'd thought Dinky really did have claustrophobia…now it was looking like an excuse. Was this something to do with last night's chat? I guessed it might be. She was freaked out about the curse, and that was linked to Ambrose, and the Hellfire Club…poor woman probably really didn't fancy spending half the day at a place that was full of reminders of all that.

Well, I was glad we were going anyway. Time for some research! I would need a pen and notepad – and hopefully, some obliging ghosts…

The Hellfire Caves

The entrance to the Hellfire Caves looked as if someone had taken the front bit of an old stone church and whacked it right into the hillside. Gothic arches stacked on top of each other, with ivy growing all over them. Looked like it had been there forever. And it seemed the caves were a pretty popular tourist attraction. There was quite a big queue.

'Oh, here we go,' said Louis, as we got in line. He pointed to the couple who were just ahead of us. 'See those guys? *Classic* suckers, bet you anything. Check it out.'

The man had a chunky build and a blond goatee beard. He wore a baseball cap and a T-shirt so huge, you could have fitted me, Sam and Floss in there with room to spare. 'Yuh, we saw it on TV, you know *Ghost World*?' he was saying in an American accent to the people in

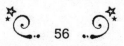

front of them. 'And we just had to check it out. They had *all* this weird stuff goin' on–'

'Yeah, there's this guy whose heart was buried here, but it got stolen,' said his girlfriend, who had dyed jet-black hair and a nose ring. 'So he wanders the caves in search of it…'

The woman they were talking to looked surprised. 'What, did you actually see the ghost on the TV show?'

'No, you don't actually *see* him,' said the American woman.

'But the ghost hunters got real freaked out, let me tell ya,' added the goatee guy. 'There was, like, strange lights an' stuff…'

'…Bad smells…'

'Real evil stuff,' he went on. "Cause these guys, these Hell-Fire dudes from the seven-teen hundreds? They were into all this devil-worship an' stuff–'

'Actually, that's a myth,' Louis chipped in.

The American turned and stared at him. "Scuse me?"

'It's a myth!' said Louis. 'Most accounts say they *didn't* practise devil-worship, actually, and there's no evidence of it anywhere. The truth is, nobody knows what the Hellfire Club did. All the members were sworn to secrecy…'

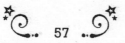

'Huh! Ain't no smoke without fire, my friend,' said goatee guy.

'Yeah! An' why keep it *secret*, if you don't got nothin' to hide?' added his girlfriend. 'They called themselves the *Hellfire Club*, man!'

'In *fact*,' said Louis, 'the Hellfire Club were all highly respected people. Benjamin Franklin!'

'What about him?'

'Ha ha, see? You didn't even know that one of your *own founding fathers* was closely involved with them. It's all in there.'

I cringed. Really, Louis could hardly be more superior if he was wearing a crown and demanding to be addressed as 'your majesty'.

The man turned his slab-like back on him. 'Oh, they were devil-worshippers, all right,' he said, like he was the authority on the matter. 'Shyeah! 'swell known – was on TV an' ev'rything.' And he and his girlfriend moved forward.

'See?' said Louis, turning to us. 'People believe what they want to believe. But those are stories, that's all.'

OK, now he was becoming just insufferable. It's not like I was especially on the Americans' side, or anything – I've seen those ghost-hunting shows, and they are *so* dumb – but right now they had my sympathy. And

Louis needed cutting down to size. 'How do you know?' I asked him.

'How do I *know?*'

'Yeah – how do you know? If this club was so secret, and there's no record of what went on...well, surely that means you can't prove the stories *aren't* true, can you?'

'Yeah!' said Emily.

Louis rolled his eyes. 'You don't get it, do you? Look, these were really important people. My ancestor was an MP – plenty of them were. They wouldn't have been Satanists! They were just having a laugh, same as we all do on Halloween.'

Just having a laugh...

I pictured those glasses flying off the shelf, all by themselves...the look of terror on Dinky's face. I thought about how she'd changed her mind about coming here. God, if the two were connected, as I thought they were...was it possible we were actually dealing with *demonic forces* here? I wasn't sure my phantorama was going to help me deal with that...

On the plus side: all of this was something I'd seen, and Louis hadn't. It felt good to know something he didn't, for once. It gave me *power.* So, with a sarcastic half-smile, I looked him squarely in the eye, and folded my arms. 'Really?' I said.

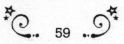

Which didn't exactly throw him off his high horse – but I did detect a wobble. A slight shadow fell across his face.

Maro returned with the tickets. She'd taken *ages*, because she'd been yakking away with Dinky's cousin Carol at the cash desk, and now she was doing the same with the Americans (classic Maro – she talks to *everybody*. Even people she's only just met, like she's known them all their lives).

So in between gabbling away, she waved our tickets at us. 'Here you are, *pethakia*, go on in! Oh, and Kitty…' She put her arm around me, and waited until the others had gone on ahead a little way. 'Is everything OK, *pethaki-mou?*' she asked.

'Er, yes, why?'

'Are you getting along all right with everyone?'

'Well…actually, Maro, would it be OK if I slept in the Hippo? The girls make a lot of noise.'

'You know, I was thinking of doing the same thing myself,' said Maro. 'I don't like to say it, but the guest bed is killing my back. I'll have an excuse to sleep in the Hippo if I'm there to keep you company. Do you feel a bit left out, *Kitaki-mou?*'

'Yeah,' I said. *Not to mention just a bit freaked out that my presence is stirring up evil spirits*, I thought grimly.

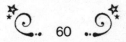

She gave me a squeeze. 'Well, we'll have each other, hmm? Hey, Carol told me this place is haunted. If you think your phantorama will make it too difficult–'

'Oh, I want to go in!' I said. 'It's no problem, there's loads of people here. I'll be fine.'

So in we went.

I could kind of see what Louis meant about cheesy. There was this crumbly aristo voice-over, telling the Story of the Caves over and over, to a background of tinny classical music. But even so, it was cool. I knew the caves were all dug out of chalk, but the walls weren't dry, flaky and white, like I imagined. The roughly hacked-out walls were all sort of darkened and waxy with age. Emily was right, it was pretty dark down there. Damp and clammy, with dirt floors.

And ghosts?

Well, I would have to see. I decided to keep away from everybody else as much as possible. Not only did the ghosts probably prefer to stay clear of the crowds (well, I was guessing that part) but if I needed to talk to one, I sure as hell didn't want anyone seeing if I could possibly help it.

It wasn't too hard, losing the others. Louis 'n' Sam, Flossie 'n' Em, were all off together…and it wasn't long before Maro got chatting with someone or other.

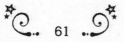

61

So I just hung back, let them go on ahead. There were other visitors, of course, but as I went further in, they kind of spread out.

I went down deeper. I came to a cavern with iron bars across it. Inside was a model of a man sitting at a desk, writing. His name was Paul Whitehead. Seemed he was the guy that Em and the American woman had mentioned, whose ghost supposedly haunted the place. A recording and a plaque beside the cavern told how it had been his dying wish to have his heart buried here in an urn. The wish was granted, but years later, someone stole the heart out of the urn – why the hell they'd want to do that, I had no idea. Poor Whitehead. If his unfinished business was getting his heart back, he didn't have a hope in hell really, did he?

Well, there was no sign of him yet. But he was a member of the Hellfire Club, so he would have known Sir Ambrose and that guy Wilkes. He could be really useful if he did turn up. That was, if I could get him to care about anything else besides his own troubles. *Did* ghosts care, I wondered? Or were they always completely self-centred? Probably. But I'd not had enough experience to know yet.

I wrote myself a note:

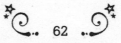

In case don't see Whitehead, ask Dinky's cousin when he was last seen in the caves.

Ha! That wouldn't be easy to do without sounding like a complete weirdo. Ah well.

I carried on. I hated to admit it, but again I could see the cheese factor Louis was on about, because there was a whole series of these caverns and in each one there were naff models of historical figures, with dusty velvet clothes, lopsided wigs and creepy grins.

A family with small kids rumbled past me down the echoing tunnel. I ran my hand along the clammy wall. I read a few other plaques, some more interesting than others. And over the centuries loads of people had carved graffiti into the soft, chalky walls. It was mostly the usual rubbish: 'Dave loves Cheryl', stuff like that. But then there were some carvings with plaques next to them – the significant bits of graffiti linked to the Hellfire Club. The Roman numeral 'XXII' was carved in one place – the plaque said nobody knew why, but there was a rumour that it had something to do with the location of a secret passage. Twenty-two what? It was anybody's guess. But I jotted it down, in case. A secret passage…now that *would* be cool.

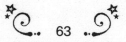

A little further along I found the number '666'. I stopped and stared. I knew only too well what that meant. 'The Mark of the Beast'. *The Devil*. I never understood *why* that number was associated with the Devil, though. No plaque alongside this one. I could just imagine Louis saying something like: 'Just because the number is there, doesn't mean it's connected to the Hellfire Club, or that they were devil-worshippers. Any idiot might have carved it.' And, of course, he'd be right. I had to stick to the facts.

Just then, a pale hand stroked the wall, close to where I was looking. 'He's late,' said a girl's voice. 'But he'll come...he will.'

I looked up. 'Oh, hello. I was wondering when one of you lot would show up.'

Land of the Dead

'He's around here somewhere. I know he is,' she said.

She was so small, shorter than me, and she can't have been more than about seventeen years old. Kind of skinny…almost pretty, but not quite.

And a ghost.

Clearly, she was a ghost. The dress was a giveaway – pale gold floor-length skirts, elbow-length sleeves with a frill of white lace hanging down from them. Blonde curls spilling from under a white mobcap, and tiny little shoulders covered in a white shawl. Her face was lit up by the candle she was carrying in a little brass holder.

'Who are you looking for?' I asked her.

Her eyes shone brightly – though they didn't really focus on me. 'We're to be married!' she announced. And her mouth widened into a huge grin. Her teeth were crooked and stained – together with the shining eyes,

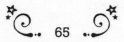

the whole effect was kind of sickly. It wasn't a happy smile, more...desperate.

Here we go again, I thought, *another ghost who can't hear me*. Obviously she was looking for her fiancé – but I could tell she wasn't answering my question, just saying stuff she'd be saying anyway. I so wanted to communicate with her, see if she could give me any clues...but it didn't look as if it was going to happen. She began trailing her fingers along the wall again, humming a tune to herself as she went. I stood back, out of her way. It was then that I saw the blood. There was a big dark patch of it on the back of her head, and the locks of hair that spilled down the back of her neck were all clagged together with it. Drips of it on the back of her shawl. I gasped...then she disappeared.

Great.

I leaned against the wall of the tunnel and took a deep breath, while another jolly group of visitors trailed past, oblivious. I carried on, but I was annoyed to find I was shaking. *Get a grip, girl.*

'Hey, Kitty!'

'Waah!' I jumped.

Then I saw that it was only Flossie – still with Emily, of course. 'We were wondering where you were,' she said. 'Hey, are you all right?'

'Yeah, I'm cool.'

'There's this bit further down you've just *got* to see,' said Emily. 'Come on!'

'Oh yeah, in a minute. But, um…you know that ghost you were talking about – the jilted bride? I think I saw a plaque about her, somewhere around here. I just wanted to…oh, here it is.'

'Sukie,' said Flossie. 'Oh, she worked in that pub we passed…'

'She was going to marry some rich guy, and got a message that he would meet her in the caves…he said they'd elope together…oh no!' I said, as I read on. 'It was a trick!'

'Ah, how horrible,' said Flossie.

'"…A cruel joke played on her by some local boys." So the message wasn't even sent by the rich guy. Oh, no… And then they came to the caves to *taunt* her about it. One of them threw a stone that… Oh!'

I couldn't bear to read out the next part, but Emily did. '"The stone hit her on the back of the head…and killed her."'

Hence the bloody mess on the back of her head. And I'd seen it. I shuddered.

'You sure you're OK?' asked Flossie.

'Yeah, really!' I took a deep breath. 'So what's this

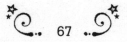

other part you want me to see, then?'

'Come on, I'll show you,' said Emily.

They led me down the tunnel until we came to a big round space with a high ceiling. A sign said it was the 'banqueting hall'. Here, recorded music played, and the walls were lined with alcoves with statues in them. Floss and Em ran along the passageway behind the alcoves, and then they were off again. It gave me a bit of time to get over the Sukie sighting. It didn't sound as if she'd be any use. But Whitehouse, or someone…surely, among all the people associated with this famously haunted place, there had to be at least one who could help me out?

After a moment or two, I heard loud giggles echoing all around, and Floss and Em appeared from the tunnel opposite. 'Don't go down there, it's really freaky!' shrieked Flossie, quite hysterical. But you could see she was loving it.

'Wait, come back!' insisted Emily, tugging on her arm. 'You haven't seen the best bit yet!'

I followed them. We had to be way deep in the ground by now, and the tunnel became a bridge over a pool of water. Here there were stalagmites and stalactites, just like in the best caves you've ever seen, and the whole thing was lit up in dramatic reds and greens. Actually, it was more like a theatrical set.

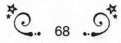

'This is the River Styx!' squeaked Flossie. 'Isn't it freaky? Just like in the Greek myths Maro tells us.'

'I know – the river that divides that land of the living from the land of the dead,' I said. 'Ha! I thought we were already in the land of the dead.'

'I knooow! That's why I don't wanna go down there!' squealed Flossie.

'But it's not scary, I promise!' insisted Emily. 'C'mon, you have to see it. It's the most secret bit of all.'

'OK, come on, let's all go,' I said, taking Flossie's hand. We went through a narrow passageway to the final cave, the 'Inner Temple'.

Here, there was a whole crowd of what looked like shop dummies: men and women. Even by eighteenth-century standards, their clothes looked like fancy dress – masks and turbans and stuff. They were made even spookier by the spotlights that lit them from below, giving them big tall shadows that loomed high up on the cave walls. Behind them was a statue of Venus, and to the right was a huge urn with some sort of ape sitting on it. The figures were grouped around a table, some sitting, some standing, and the table was set with a candelabra, pewter tankards and fake goblets of wine. They looked like they were having a right old party.

'Ooh, they creep me out, Em!' cried Flossie, who

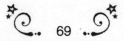

I reckoned was completely carried away with the *idea* of being creeped out.

'Me too!' shrieked Emily. 'Isn't it great?'

There was a recording on a loop that told a bizarre story about one of the Hellfire Club meetings. My ears pricked up when I heard the name John Wilkes – apparently, one of the figures was meant to be him.

'Wilkes is supposed to have dressed a baboon as the devil,' went the recording. 'He hid it in a chest, then released it. The poor frightened creature then jumped on the back of Lord Sandwich…'

'Lord Sandwich!' gasped Flossie. 'They named a lord after a *sandwich*?' She and Emily dissolved into fits of giggles again.

'No, silly, it's the other way round,' I said. 'He *invented* the sandwich. Everyone knows that.'

The girls just went on giggling. 'Lord Ham Sandwich! Lord Cheese-and-Pickle Sandwich!'

'Oh, listen to this bit,' said Emily, as the voice-over quoted Lord Sandwich's reaction: 'Oh, spare me, gracious devil! Though knowest I was only fooling. I'm not *half* as wicked as I *pretend*!'

'He thought it really was the devil!' said Emily, and she and Flossie fell about laughing.

I wasn't laughing.

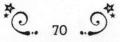

For one thing, I couldn't help thinking: give me a break. How *old* were these guys?! What a way for grown men to behave. But mostly I was thinking about what the story told me about the Hellfire Club meetings.

'How would Louis explain that, then?' I wondered aloud.

'Huh?'

'Well, if, like Louis said, the Hellfire gang weren't involved in any kind of devil-worship…then what exactly was Lord Sandwich trying to cover up? Why would he admit to wickedness – even just pretend wickedness – to this "devil"? Sure sounds to *me* like they were up to something.'

'Oh, Louis says it's just a *story*,' said Emily. 'You're not meant to take it seriously. Hey, and do you see the one with the red waistcoat?'

'Yeah.'

'Apparently that's meant to be my ancestor, Sir Ambrose. It's hard to tell 'cause he's not wearing his wig. But if you look close, you can see it looks like him. Same nose and everything. Come on, Floss.'

And off they went again across the Styx, giggling. I stayed behind, staring at the Sir Ambrose figure, Lord Sandwich…and that other devil, Wilkes – he just had to be the one in the white wig and blue jacket. Man, he was

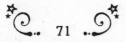

ugly. I mean, all of them were creepy as hell, but this Wilkes dummy had a particularly leery grin and these big, staring eyes, which were badly painted, making it look as if he had a squint.

'Well, you're a right laugh, aren't you,' I found myself saying to him out loud, hands on my hips. I did feel a bit sorry for Lord Sandwich, but I felt even more sorry for the poor baboon. Jeez. I guessed back in those days people were desperate for a bit of fun, what with there being no telly and all that. People probably goofed off all the time. Still, not very nice. Although nothing compared to putting a *curse* on someone.

I hung around for a bit longer, while other people came and went. Because this Inner Temple was clearly the key spot. If you imagined the Hellfire Caves as a planet, it was like this was its fiery centre. So if any part of the caves was likely to be haunted, surely this would be it.

And who was most likely to haunt it? Hopefully the one with unfinished business, of course: Sir Ambrose. I knew that Sir Ambrose must be haunting *somewhere*, and since that somewhere didn't appear to be Dinky's house, then this might just be it. I gazed at his dummy – which did feel kind of dumb. But it helped me to focus my thoughts on him.

'Hey Kit,' said Sam.

I turned around with a start. 'Oh, hi.'

'What do you think? Pretty cheesy, huh?'

'Sam, you sound exactly like Louis,' I said. 'Stop it.'
I went back to staring at Sir Ambrose.

'Hey, there you are. It's time to go.' Louis' voice
came echoing down the tunnel.

'No! I'm not ready,' I said.

'Yeah, but–'

'I'll meet you at the entrance, OK? I promise I won't
be long.'

'Oh-kay,' said Louis. 'C'mon, Sam.'

I watched the two of them go, then went back to
concentrating on Sir Ambrose. As I turned, I noticed a
small movement in the corner of my eye. I froze.
Without moving my head, I shifted my gaze – it seemed
as if it had come from where the Wilkes figure was
sitting. Did I imagine that? I stood and stared at the
dummy, almost going cross-eyed myself from staring so
hard. Then–

His head lifted, and he winked at me.

No! That wasn't possible. It was a *dummy*, for
heaven's sake. Then something even stranger happened.

The head sort of…shimmered. It looked – well, it
looked *alive*. Then its features kind of smeared across its

73

face – like it was looking in two directions at once. Two faces, one layered on top of the other. One looking towards the table, and the other looking at me. And grinning, the most *horrible* squinty grin, with gappy, tombstone teeth.

I felt a lurch of horror deep in my gut. I couldn't move. I'd stopped breathing, and my mouth was dry as paper. Then the grin went away, and the dummy's head returned to normal.

Some more people came down the tunnel – Mr Goatee and his girlfriend among them. 'Now, this part here? People have reported some real *sinister sensations* down here,' Mr Goatee was telling his companions. 'It's not something you can see or hear. It's just...a sense of evil. D'you feel it?'

Evil. Was that what I'd just experienced? Is that what had chilled me to the bone?

Flying Books

I saw something. I wasn't imagining it, I know I wasn't. And I sensed a presence, too. And I think it was Wilkes himself, the old trickster. OK – bring it on. If I can't get hold of the spirit of Sir Ambrose (although WHY not??! Doesn't it BOTHER him that his descendants are still suffering the effects of the curse?) then here's what I need to do: get back to the Hellfire Caves somehow, and make contact with Wilkes.

Only…would that be completely nuts?

Got to admit, am just a LEETLE bit freaked out by the idea. Dealing with someone who set a powerful curse – one that's lasted for CENTURIES – that kind of has a

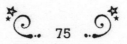

huge sign on it saying AVOID, doesn't it? Run away! Don't be messing with the black magic stuff, you're going to one BAD place there. Hmm. But the trouble with signs saying 'avoid' is they only make you want to go there more…

'I hope Dinky doesn't take this personally,' I said to Maro, as she and I moved our stuff back into the Hippo.

'Oh, no, not at all,' said Maro. 'She understands, *kamari-mou*.'

'OK, good.' Yeah. No doubt Dinky could see for herself that I was the odd one out, and no amount of Cluedo games was going to fix that. Emily had been a bit of a problem, suddenly deciding that *she* really wanted to sleep in the Hippo as well, but that would've defeated the object – well, one of them, anyway. Fortunately, Dinky took her aside and managed to knock that idea on the head.

The only other issue was putting Maro's mind at rest, 'cause while we were putting our stuff away in the Hippo, she kept going, 'Is anything troubling you at the house?' and all that.

'I'm fine,' I said. 'I told you, it's just all the noise the girls make.'

'What about that "strange atmosphere" you felt?' said

Maro. 'Have you seen any ghosts yet?'

'No, I haven't,' I said. Which was true.

So – peace and quiet. I hoped.

Only that's not how it turned out. Somehow I just couldn't settle down. After a while, I realised that this was actually my first night in the Hippo. So even though my neat little flip-down bed was actually really comfortable, had a nifty bedside light and everything, I guess it's just that I wasn't used to it yet. And I couldn't stop thinking about what I'd seen, down there in the caves. Every time I managed to get the leering face of John Wilkes out of my mind, Sukie would appear with her sickly smile and bloodied head.

Then I heard a sort of rumbling noise. I sat up. Nothing for a moment...then again: *rumble rumble rumble* – like the sound of a truck going by. I got up and went to the window. There was nothing to see out there, but when the sound came again, I got a better sense of where it was, and whaddya know? It was coming from the house. I was sure of it. *Hmm.* So much for removing myself and making things better.

Well, if there was going to be disturbance anyway, I might as well investigate it. Silently, I slipped into my hi-tops and pulled on my hoody. I took the keys from the hook by the door, then hesitated.

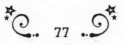

Hetty. She might freak out if she saw someone lurking about. But I didn't have anything to give her… I'd just have to hope she'd be OK once she knew it was me. I stepped outside, shutting the door as quietly as possible. I crept right up to the house, close to the living room window at the front. But the curtains were drawn, so there was nothing to see…then came the rumbling noise again – louder this time. I snuck around the side of the house, pulling my hoody tightly around me; it was chilly. The kitchen had French windows, so I could get a good view inside. But then the rumble came again, and the noise didn't seem to be coming from there. It was the living room, I reckoned. And the only way I'd be able to see anything in there was if I got inside the house.

I tried the French windows: locked. Then I checked the other windows, and found one that wasn't quite closed all the way. The sash slid open, smooth as butter.

I could hear Hetty growling. I pushed my head through the curtains and saw her waddling over, about as threatening as a doped-up sheep. 'Hello, Hetty,' I whispered. Reaching in as far as I could, I patted her on the head and scratched her between the ears. She was happy. I stomach-shuffled my way in, and tumbled onto the living room couch. I shut the window.

So – I was in. Now what?

I waited. As my eyes got used to the darkness, I kept them peeled for the slightest movement. I didn't like that there were still gloomy corners that I couldn't see into…I couldn't help imagining what might be lurking there. I didn't like that the bronze statue of a boy on the table beside me was leering up at me, like a naughty imp. But after a few minutes, tiredness crept up on me. It was cosy, there on the couch. And dark, and quiet. Only the faint sound of someone coughing upstairs punctured the silence. I curled up with Hetty and waited.

I was about to drop off, when there it was again: the rumbling noise. Actually, more of a sort of rumble-rattle. Then I saw that the antique dresser on the other side of the room was kind of…shuddering. Hetty stopped snoring abruptly, sat up and stared. As the dresser wobbled, its glass doors glimmered in the dim light.

Hetty whimpered. I patted her head. 'Sshh, it's OK,' I whispered. I got up, tiptoed across the room and shut the door. 'Who's there?' I asked in the loudest whisper I felt I could get away with.

Nothing.

The dresser began vibrating again. Now that I was closer, I could see that there was a little key in the glazed door, and an invisible force was wiggling it about. Then a drawer was yanked open. Then another one.

'Ambrose?' I tried. 'Is that you?' But the dresser just shuddered even more, and now the stuff that was in the drawers – coasters, papers, pens, a magnifying glass, a small sewing kit – started flying out all over the place.

'OK, stop that!' I called out, dodging the flying missiles. 'Just…whatever it is that's making you angry… maybe I can help!' I narrowly missed being whacked on the head by a tin of peppermints. Could he/she/it hear me? I had no idea. I just had to keep on trying.

'Please talk to me!' I said, ducking another missile.

Hetty started whimpering. I went over and crouched next to her, stroked and comforted her. It helped a bit, but she was still freaked out. I could see the whites of her eyes, poor thing.

There was silence for a moment. Then the key started rattling in the keyhole again. Then: rattle, rattle, *thwack!* The glazed doors burst open, and the books inside began to fly out, one by one. The books were antiques themselves, hardbacks with gold embossed lettering. Their pages fluttered as they sailed through the air.

I backed off and huddled behind an armchair with Hetty, not knowing what the hell to do. One thing seemed pretty obvious: whoever or whatever was doing this couldn't care less about me and my phantorama. But then, maybe they just needed help connecting – and

I wasn't making that any easier by hiding behind the chair.

I stuck my head out. 'OK, I'm going to give you one more chance! Just...stop what you're doing, and talk to me!'

And right then, the books stopped flying out of the cabinet.

Wow.

I took a deep breath. 'OK! Great! Thank you. Now...can I see you, please? I don't like talking to the furniture, it makes me feel stupid.'

The room was deathly silent. Again, all I could hear was the occasional bout of coughing from upstairs. And I thought I heard a floorboard creak up there. How would I explain myself to Dinky, if she came down to investigate? I decided I couldn't worry about that. If I could rid this house of its curse, she wouldn't care, would she? She'd just be ecstatically grateful. *If* I could, that is. On the other hand, if I *couldn't*...

'OK, I'm waiting,' I said. I stared hard into the gloomy space. I still couldn't see anything, but...there was that *feeling*. The sense I got when a presence was emerging, when a spirit was about to appear. Like the way you can know someone's entered the room, even if you haven't seen or heard them. Sometimes there's a smell, too...I thought I smelled something smoky, like

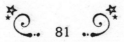

a bonfire. 'Yes, yes – come on!' I said. 'I can feel you!'

Then, suddenly, whatever it was just…went. Like a flame going out. The smoky smell hung around, but the presence was gone.

Another cough, another creak from upstairs.

Hetty got up and started sniffing around.

'Did you feel it too, Het?' I whispered. I got up and looked at the books strewn across the floor and on the armchairs. I started picking them up and quietly putting them back. Some of them were seriously old. History books. Charlie was into all that stuff: British kings and queens…the Plantagenets, the Tudors. And wars. Blimey, I thought, why would anyone actually *choose* to read this stuff? Too much like school.

'Oh well,' I sighed, as I was about to put another book away. 'Maybe next time, eh?'

Then all of a sudden, the presence was back. An invisible force yanked the book out of my hand.

'Aargh!' I cried. I stared in disbelief as it hovered in midair. The pages flipped over, back and forth. Then one page was ripped out, crumpled and thrown at my feet. The book was once again flung to the floor; then the whole dresser began shuddering again, the doors flapping wildly. The delicate glass panes began to shatter as the doors slammed and slammed repeatedly…now

I saw that the top of the dresser was leaning forward – the whole thing was about to collapse.

Hetty began barking wildly. There was nothing for it: picking up the crumpled page, I dived for the window, and scrambled out as quickly as I could – just as the whole dresser came smashing down.

I got back to the Hippo without anyone seeing me.

'Hmm? *Ti einai*…whazzat?' asked Maro sleepily.

I froze.

Then she started babbling on in Greek, and I could tell she wasn't really awake. She soon settled. I found a small torch in a drawer in the kitchenette. I snuck over to my bed, got under the covers and uncrumpled the page from the book. The title at the top was *The Seven Years' War*, and on it was an illustration, a drawing of a seated man. A very ugly man, with a long pole leaning against his shoulder, and some sort of bell-shaped thing on top with the word 'Liberty' written on it. He had this revolting, leering grin, and his eyeballs were turned in towards his nose. He had stumpy tombstone teeth and a huge, jutting jaw.

Underneath was his name:

John Wilkes, Esq.

The Thing

OMG, is that ever one fearsome poltergeist/ghost/demon/whatever, lurking at Dinky's house. My heart is still pumping, and I can hear voices from the house. Poor Dinky. She was already freaked out as it was, and now it's her FURNITURE that's getting thrown around. So much for me removing myself and making things calm down. But then, maybe I haven't gone far enough away – plus I'm there during the day.

So now it's even more important for me to help – if I can. In fact, at this point I'm thinking I have a MORAL OBLIGATION.

And I've been given a CLUE.

A very strange portrait of John Wilkes. Only…what does it tell me? I knew about Wilkes already. Maybe there are more clues in the picture. Ah, I don't know…so tired…

Dinky looked white as a sheet the next morning.

The dresser was back in its place, minus several panes of glass. Dinky and Charlie were on their knees in the living room, tidying up the books and other stuff that had been flung around the room. Still, she tried to be all bright and jolly but the strain was showing more than ever.

'Are you all right, Dinky?' asked Maro.

Dinky sat back on her heels, took a big slug of coffee and gave a fake grin. 'Oh, I'm fine! Just barely slept, that's all. We had another accident…'

'Can you believe it?' said Charlie, also doing the fake-jolly thing. 'You'd think we'd know better than to cram so many heavy books into this dresser. Damn thing was much too top-heavy!'

'Yes, and poor old Hetty was terrified,' added Dinky. 'She must've just brushed against it, and whoosh – down it came!'

'And Em's really sick,' said Flossie.

'Yes, she's got some sort of chest thing,' said Dinky.

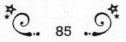

'Nasty cough, and a really high temperature. I've been up half the night with her.'

'Oh no!' I said. 'Is she in bed?'

'Asleep in our room now,' said Dinky.

'And I'm to stay away from her,' said Flossie, miserably.

'I'm sorry, sweetie,' said Dinky. 'But we don't want you getting sick as well.'

I felt a stab of fear run through me. Illness…that would be the next thing, wouldn't it – if the curse was growing stronger all over again? It was what happened to Sir Ambrose himself. Of course, it was possible that my presence was not the thing that was disturbing the spirits – it was even possible that Emily had just got sick, nothing to do with the curse. But did I really want to take a gamble on that?

Maro looked worried. 'Oh, Dinky, I think we'd better give you some space,' she said. 'You've got so much on your plate.'

'No, no!' Dinky began. Then she paused. 'Well, I…'

I thought quickly. Although I needed to get right away from the house, the thought of having to drop my investigation into the curse just when things were starting to look hopeful was *really* frustrating. 'I think Maro's right,' I said. 'But I remember seeing a campsite just along

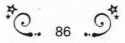

the river from here. We could stay there, maybe?'

'Oh, that's a good idea,' said Maro. 'I've got a bunch of field trips I was planning in the area anyway – all part of the home-schooling.'

'Ah, OK,' said Dinky. 'But…the campsite costs money…oh, I do feel bad. Let me give you something–'

'*Asti!* Stop!' commanded Maro, holding her hands up. 'Emily is sick, my dear, you can't help that. And like I say, we won't be far away, we can still see each other. And Emily can join in when she's better. OK?'

Dinky and Charlie looked at each other. 'OK,' said Dinky at last.

So that morning we took the Hippo over to the campsite. And since we were giving Dinky's family a bit of breathing space, we made ourselves some lunch – our first one in the Hippo! It was kind of fun. Everything in the Hippo is so dinky – and *not* in the way that Dinky is! It's cosy, with a kid-sized kitchen and everything. Makes you feel almost like you're playing house, only it's for real. After that we went out by ourselves – on one of Maro's field trips, making notes about local landmarks and stuff. School work, basically. Yeah, it was a Sunday, but we knew that was the deal, 'cause we were getting other days off when most kids were in school. It was OK, actually, and good to have Sam and Flossie's

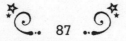

company again. I'd started to miss them.

Maro came alongside me and hugged me to her as we walked. She started up about that 'strange atmosphere' over at Dinky's house again, and had I seen any ghosts?

I kept my head down as we tramped along the soggy riverside. 'Nope,' I said. 'Still nothing.'

I really couldn't go into it. I certainly wasn't going to let on what I'd overheard Dinky telling her – or that I'd snuck into the house at night.

'What do you think it was, then – this strange atmosphere?' asked Maro.

Sam hovered nearby, listening in.

I shrugged. 'I don't know. Sometimes I think you get ghosts that are just sort of…not really one thing or the other. Neither exactly there or not. I guess that's what's going on in Dinky's house.' How convincing did that sound? I had no idea.

Maro sighed. 'Well, just tell me if you do see anything, sweetie. I…I don't think all is well there.'

Some old building Of Historical Interest appeared on the other side of the river, and Maro switched to Lesson Mode, telling us all about it. So that was that…for now.

After lunch, Sam arranged to join Louis and his Insula Club pals on the island, and Maro and Flossie

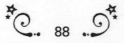

asked me to go clothes shopping with them.

'Er, I've got enough stuff at the moment, thanks,' I said. I didn't fancy it. I mean, I love clothes and all that, it's just that I liked the junky stuff in the markets in our old neighbourhood. Maro and Flossie were going to some revolting suburban mall – *ick*.

'Please come, Kitty,' said Flossie. 'What else are you going to do?'

'She could come with me,' suggested Sam.

I yawned. 'I'm too tired. I hardly got any sleep last night. I'll just stay here.'

'Oh, come on, Kitty, you don't want to just sit around here with nothing to do,' said Maro. 'We'll all be gone for hours.'

I chewed on my lip. She was right; I probably would get bored and lonely after a while. If only I could visit the caves; that was where I really wanted to go. Find a way of sneaking in…see if that Wilkes ghost would appear again…see if I could connect with him. Ah, who was I kidding? Had I ever once had a proper conversation with a ghost? Things were developing all the time, and it still might happen…but it hadn't yet. Besides, I didn't know how to get there.

So: mall or island? Boredom or humiliation? It was a tough call. But maybe those boys just had to be

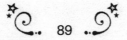

confronted after all. Wimping out wasn't the answer, I decided. 'OK,' I said. 'I'll go with Sam.'

'We'll need our bikes, then,' said Sam.

'Bravo! *Endaksi*,' said Maro. She got our bikes off the rack at the back of the Hippo, then she and Flossie left.

'OK, Kit,' said Sam, the moment they were out of earshot. 'You know what Maro was asking you earlier? Come on, you can tell me. There so blatantly *is* a ghost in Dinky's house – right?'

I sighed. I was used to sharing everything with Sam – it felt strange not to. 'No, not a ghost – not exactly,' I said at last. 'Look, I'll tell you on the way. But you're not to breathe a word of this to *anyone*. Promise?'

'I promise.'

We left the campsite on a footpath through an open field. There wasn't a soul in sight. We got off our bikes and walked with them. 'OK, here it is,' I said. 'There's a curse on the family.'

Sam looked at me and burst out laughing. 'Don't be daft, Kit. That's ancient history!'

This took me by surprise. 'You know about it?'

"Course I do. Louis told me all about it, after I asked him why Dinky got all funny about the house burning down and everything. He says she's a bit weird about her ancestor for some reason. Doesn't like to talk about

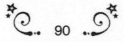

what happened to him.'

'Yeah well, there's a very *good reason* for that,' I said. 'The curse is still active.'

I told him everything I'd overheard Dinky tell Maro, and about the flying objects and crashing furniture. 'Those stories she told about the shelf coming down, and the cabinet collapsing because it was weighed down with too many books? All lies. She just doesn't want the rest of us to know what's really going on.'

Sam was silent.

'Sam? What are you thinking?'

'I don't know, Kit. I'm...I'm shocked. Curses? Demons? No, this is crazy. There must be a rational explanation for what's going on. I know Dinky thinks it's the curse, but...maybe she's like, *losing it.*'

'Dinky's not crazy.'

'No? Strikes me, she's getting a bit loopy.'

'OK, did you believe what Louis told you about what the curse did to Sir Ambrose or not?'

'Not really. I mean, it was like, *centuries* ago. Stuff gets exaggerated like crazy.'

'So? What difference does that make? This is *real*, Sam: I saw it happen with my own eyes. And now Emily's ill. For all we know, that could be down to the curse as well.'

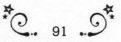

'Well, good job we got the hell out of there, I say.'

'So Louis doesn't know what's been going on the last couple of days?'

'If he does, he hasn't told me anything.'

'All right, well, now you know why I was so keen to get out of there. But it isn't just about escaping; it's about damage limitation. I think the spirit sensed me – I was making it more agitated. Maybe things will calm down a bit, now I'm completely gone. All the same, I still want to help somehow. I think I'm meant to.'

'Oh, Kit, no–'

'No, I am! I've been given a message. Look.' I pulled out the picture of John Wilkes, quickly showed it to him, then shoved it back in my pocket. 'This was *ripped out* of a book, right in front of me. If that isn't a message, I don't know what is.'

'What the…? Kit, you don't know what you're dealing with here! We're out of there now. You should just drop it.'

'*Drop* it?'

'Yeah. I think you're right: whether it's evil spirits or the ghost of Sir Ambrose causing this – or both – it figures that they sensed the presence of someone with phantorama. It would certainly explain why there's much more trouble now, after a month of just stupid

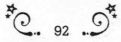

colanders going missing and stuff. So now you've removed yourself. Problem solved.'

'Well, hardly,' I said. 'Things are still going to go missing, aren't they?'

'Shock! Horror!' said Sam. 'They'll live with it. Just more evidence of Dinky losing her marbles, if you ask me.'

'Dinky is *not* losing her marbles! God, you're sounding like Louis again.'

'What are you talking about? I've not heard him say his mum's off her trolley.'

'Don't be so literal, Sam. What I mean is… Oh, forget it. Anyway, Dinky might not be crazy *yet*, but she'll soon get that way if this carries on. I think I'd go pretty bonkers if I was constantly trying to…'

'Trying to what?'

'Trying to find something… Sam, that's it, don't you see? The *thing*. I'd almost forgotten!'

'The thing?'

'What Dinky said – the thing Sir Ambrose has been searching for all this time – whatever it was that Wilkes stole, to put the curse on him. Ambrose is still searching for it and it's driving him crazy. *That's* his unfinished business. If I can find the thing, and bring it back to the family…maybe that's all it would take to lift the curse!'

Initiation Rite

We cycled to the village and over the bridge to the main picnic island, where Louis had arranged to collect us in his boat. Sam still insisted I should just leave things alone. Ha! Boys. Think they're so brave, when really it's us girls who've got all the guts.

Eventually I gave up trying to convince him. We walked down to the water's edge, and waited for Louis. 'So what do I have to do for this stupid Insula Club initiation, anyway?' I asked.

'Oh, Kit, I'm really sorry, but I can't tell you that,' said Sam. 'It's against the rules.'

'What? Oh, give me a break! I let you into the secret of the curse, now it's your turn. C'mon – spill.'

Sam looked deadly serious. 'It's a question of honour, Kit.'

'Don't give me that. I'm your sister!'

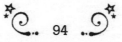

'It doesn't work like that, Kitty…you don't break the bond. Not under any circumstances. You didn't have to swear an oath. I did. That's the difference.'

OK, if I was annoyed before, I was getting majorly irritated now. 'You know, Sam, you so need to get over yourself. You just admire Louis way too much. Honestly, it makes me want to *vomit*.'

'I do not!' protested Sam. 'It's got nothing to do with admiration. It's a point of principle, that's all… Anyway, shut up. Look, he's here.'

Great. Mystery initiation rite, here I come.

Again I stumbled trying to do that nonchalant leaping-off-the-boat thing, and *again* I felt about this high. Just by setting foot on that island, I already felt like an inferior being.

'OK, so since you're here, Kitty, let's get you initiated,' said Louis. He grinned. Had this little stick he was chewing on. I could feel his friends Jonah and Joss looking me up and down, convinced I was going to fail. Creeps.

All right – bring it on. I was ready. I couldn't have cared less about acceptance into their stupid club, but there was a battle to be won here. I stared Louis right in the eye. 'OK.'

'First thing is the obstacle course,' said Louis.

95

Oh wow, how predictable.

'No problem,' I said.

There was a rope stretched between the branches of two trees several metres apart – a thick rope, tightly knotted, sturdy and taut.

Louis pointed with his little stick. 'You have to get across there, monkey-bar style. Then, see that other rope hanging down? You have to use that to swing to the next tree. At the top of that tree I've hung a canvas bag. Climb up to it. Inside the bag you'll find an apple. You have to carry the apple between your teeth while you walk along the log, then jump the stepping stones – no touching the ground, or you'll have to go right back to the beginning. Then the really fun bit is at the end – but we'll talk about that when you get there. Oh, and you get to eat the apple afterwards.'

'Right,' I said. 'Great.'

I'm not a bad tree-climber as it happens – but I was a bit out of practice. And this tree looked discouragingly tall and lacking in footholds. Well, I had to give it my best shot. I spat on my palms and rubbed my hands together, then threw myself onto the trunk of the tree, clamping hard with hands, elbows, knees and feet. Deep breath…I hoisted myself up. It was hard at first, but then I got into the rhythm of it. I could feel I was getting

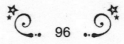

scraped all over the place, but I had to just ignore the stinging pain and carry on. I reached up and grabbed the rope. Another deep breath. Then I hauled up my other hand and let myself fall away from the tree, swinging free.

'That's it!' cried Sam, trying to be all supportive now. *Shut up.*

I thrashed my legs about, propelling my way along the rope, little by little. God, did it cut into my hands! It *burned*, like fire and ice.

I kept going.

Just…kept…on…going. By the time I was three-quarters of the way there, it felt like my arms were about to come out of their sockets and my hands were flaming. Finally, I got to hurl myself onto the branch of the other tree. Couldn't help letting out a really loud grunt as I did so. *Yes!* First hurdle, a little light applause. Thank you, thank you. And for my next trick…

More deep breaths. Sitting here, I could rest a bit. I was sweating now. I took off my hoody and tied it round my waist. I looked up and saw the canvas bag dangling from an upper branch. The limb I'd have to climb to get there was again thin on footholds, and covered with moss; it would be slippery. My hands were *screaming* at me, but I had to just carry on – no wimping out now.

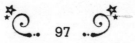

I reached up to the next branch, hoisted myself up –
then slipped right back down again. 'Ow!'

'You all right?' called Louis.

God, this was humiliating. 'Yeah,' I cried out, hoping
he didn't hear the wobble in my voice. I soothed my
hand under my armpit. But it wasn't the mossy bark that
had made me slip – it was a surprise.

Because all of a sudden, there, dangling his little legs
from the branch above me, sat a boy. He had curly blond
hair and wore a blue jacket and breeches, like something
straight out of a Victorian soap advertisement. He was
swinging his legs and humming to himself, peeling away
at one of those little propeller-like seed-pods.

He smiled down at me. 'It's great up here, isn't it?'

I just nodded. I really wanted to answer – there was
always the possibility that *this* one would at last be the
ghost that would hear me and actually answer back. But
I couldn't say anything; the boys would think I was
talking to myself. Really, this was highly inconvenient!
So not the right time for a phantorama encounter. And he
was extra distracting, because he was so sweet-looking
and no more than about six years old – and he'd probably
died as a result of an accident right around here.

Don't think about that! I told myself. Just try to
ignore him.

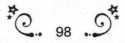

I hoisted myself back up again, climbing higher until I was above the ghost – who went on humming happily to himself – and the canvas bag loomed closer. I reached the base of the branch it was attached to – at last! This bit would be easier. I swung my leg over and shimmied along on my bum. But then the branch got perilously narrow and began to droop under my weight, so I lay flat on my stomach and stretched out my arm as far as I could. Then I got this tickling sensation in my armpit.

'Aah!' I cried, yanking my arm back. Looking down, I saw the little boy-ghost, giggling as he reached up, waving a pigeon feather.

'Stop that!' I snapped.

'Stop what?' asked Sam.

'You want to stop?' asked Louis.

Oh, jeez…

'No!' I yelled back. 'It was…a fly was bothering me, that's all.'

What were you supposed to do about harassment from ghosts? It was so unfair! They could do what they liked to me, but nothing I did back ever seemed to have any effect. Plus, I had to avoid looking like a complete lunatic.

So in the end I just glared at Little Boy Blue, as if to say, 'don't even *think* about doing that again', and

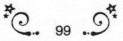

reached out again for the bag. I looped my finger under the handles and brought it down. I looked again, and now Little Boy Blue was gone. Good.

Next up: the apple. I got it out of the bag, and, wedging it between my teeth, I shimmied back down the branch, the limb, and the trunk of the tree, then dropped down onto the log. Sweet juices dripped from the apple onto my tongue; I felt my mouth tingle, and saliva dribbled down my chin. It was driving me crazy, but I just had to ignore it and carry on.

I was beginning to wonder what final delight Louis had in store for me, when my nose gave me a clue: wood-smoke. And there was the crackling sound of a fire. Oh wow.

'OK, you're nearly there,' said Louis. 'Last thing is–' He paused, and I could swear he was suppressing a snigger. 'Jumping over the bonfire. Think you can do that?'

Well, I couldn't answer, could I? I still had that apple wedged between my teeth, and drool all down my chin. Nice. I could feel the rage rise inside me as I hopped from log to stepping-stone, and onto the next. In the corner of my eye, I thought I glimpsed a low-flying bird or something. A second or so later, I realised what it was when the air filled with a revolting smell like rotten eggs.

Someone had chucked a stink bomb.

Cue cries of disgust as the breeze drifted the smell in the boys' direction.

'Argh, *Jonah!*' cried Louis.

At the same time, the boys were all cracking up with laughter, except Sam. 'That wasn't fair,' he said.

'Sorry,' said Jonah, not sounding sorry at all.

I was glad at least Sam thought it was out of order, but there was no undoing it now, and the smell just made the whole thing unbearable. *Why* had I agreed to put myself through this? I felt like a performing animal in the circus. But the adrenalin was pumping through my veins like crazy – there was no stopping now.

And here I was, at the bonfire. It danced on the spot, lashing out this way and that in the wind. My jaw was killing me, and now a really awful image popped into my head: a roast suckling pig, rotating slowly over the fire with an apple in its mouth, its skin blistering. *Yummy*.

Sam hopped along close by. 'It's easier than it looks, Kit,' he said. 'The speed of your movement blows the flames out of the way.'

Yeah, thanks for the advice, bro. The hottest part of the flame is the tip!

As I sized up the fire and tried to work out a strategy, I saw again, wobbling in the heat haze, the face of Little

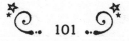

Boy Blue. Still laughing, but the distortion made his angelic features seem cruel and mocking – more like a little devil.

I took a deep breath, making a slooshing noise through my wedged-open, saliva-filled mouth. I wanted to yell but of course I couldn't – all that came out was a sort of screech-growl…and I threw myself over.

There was searing, unbearable heat and for a terrible moment I thought my shorts had caught fire but then…then I was on the ground, and not on fire, just a crumpled, aching heap.

I spat out the apple.

I'd done it.

I lay there, staring up at the treetops as the boys applauded me. But I didn't feel pleased – I was furious.

Louis stood over me, chewing on his stick. 'Hey, you made it. Well done!' How was it that even when congratulating me on doing something *extraordinary*, he still managed to sound so underwhelmed?

'I *really* didn't think she would,' muttered one of his friends.

I propped myself up on my elbows and wiped my face on my sleeve.

Sam crouched beside me. 'You OK, Kitty?'

'I'm *fine*,' I said, through gritted teeth.

'Good,' said Louis. 'So, you ready for the final challenge?'

'The *what*?'

'We're not done yet,' said Louis. 'There's still the "Insula's Got Talent" challenge. You can sing, dance, tell jokes…whatever you want, really.'

The other boys smirked.

What? Oh, this was too much now. I felt the rage expand inside me like a shaken-up soda drink. So it wasn't enough that I had literally jumped through fire; now I was expected to sing and dance as well? Grabbing the apple, I stood up and hurled it at Louis. 'Whatever!' I yelled. 'I don't even care about your stupid club. I just wanted to prove I could do it!'

Sam stepped forward, trying to soothe me. 'Hey, hey…'

Louis had dodged the apple and was still grinning. 'All right, it's just a bit of fun,' he said. 'Don't take it so seriously.' He leaned against a tree, nonchalantly picking his teeth with that stick of his. 'But don't join if you don't want to, 's OK by me.'

Something fell heavy and sour in my gut. Still, after all that…*still* he wasn't impressed. Just what did it take to cut this boy down to size? But no way was I going to perform some stupid variety act for him, even if I was

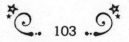

any good at that sort of thing. Which I wasn't. But the alternative was to ditch the whole thing...and then it would be Louis 1, Kitty 0. No, I'd have to do something.

I racked my brains. *Talent*...well, a talent could be any number of things, couldn't it? And what talent did I have...?

'Ah, waste of time,' said Jonah. 'She's not gonna do it.' They wandered off a little way.

'No, I am,' I said at last.

The boys turned around.

'Only...this is something a bit different from what you're expecting.'

Louis raised an eyebrow. 'Oh?'

I stepped forward, hoping he couldn't see that I was shaking. What I proposed to say was a massive gamble, in more ways than one, but...I just had to go for it. 'I'm going to lift your family curse.'

'Kitty!' Sam looked shocked.

Louis, for once, was dumbfounded. Then, as I expected, he burst out laughing. 'What the hell are you talking about? There's no curse!'

My turn to act superior. 'Oh no? Then what's causing things to go missing? Glasses to get smashed, furniture to fall down...maybe even your sister to get sick?'

'Oh, come on, that's not—'

'Some things can't be explained, Louis. You think you know everything, but you don't.'

'Really?' Louis folded his arms. He looked at his friends, then back at me. 'Well, if it's something that can't even be explained, then how, *exactly*, do you propose to put an end to it?'

Good question!

'I don't have to tell you my methods,' I said. 'All I will tell you is that it involves a stolen object that belonged to your ancestor, Sir Ambrose Vyner. It was taken for the casting of the curse.' I could feel Sam's eyes burning into me, but I ignored him. 'Once it's returned to the family,' I went on, 'the curse will be lifted. Life will go back to normal.' I was just blagging at this point, of course, didn't have a clue how I'd actually achieve all this. But I was on a roll now, couldn't stop myself.

Louis stared at me, then burst out laughing again. 'Oh, brilliant! This I've gotta see. Whoo! We're in a Stephen King movie. Well, hey, bring it on, Kitty. So…you'll produce this object, whatever it is? And that'll be your, uh, *proof*?'

'Yup. Oh, but can I have a bit of time? I can't just magic it out of thin air.'

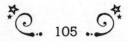

Louis stared at me, fascinated. 'Sure,' he said, flipping his little stick over his shoulder. 'Take all the time you need.'

Little Boy Blue scampered right past him. Not a leaf stirred.

Illness

We hung out at the house for just a short while, then headed back to the campsite in the early evening. Poor Emily was still really sick. I wondered what surprises tonight would bring…although I still hoped my absence would improve the situation.

While Floss was helping Maro get supper ready, I took a quick shower, then went outside to dress my wounds from the initiation. Obviously I didn't want Maro or Flossie to see or there would be too many questions.

Sam came out. 'Kitty.'

I ignored him, just went on dabbing my knee with antiseptic.

'Ouch.' Sam winced. 'You OK?'

'Yeah…sss!' I screwed up my eyes as I tried to deal with the stinging. This was the first chance I'd had to

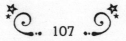

clean them up properly. I'd done what I could at Dinky's, then just covered my cuts and bruises with the jeans and big sloppy sweater I'd brought to change into. Those sleeves had been good for covering my hands, too.

A little packet of something landed by my side. 'What's that…stink bombs?'

'Yeah. Peace offering. Thought you might want to get your own back some time.'

'Oh…thanks.' I pocketed them.

''S OK. That was out of order. But…god, Kitty – lift the curse? What were you *thinking*?'

'I had a point to prove! And no way was I going to do some stupid song or dance.'

'But how the hell are you going to do it?'

I didn't look at him, just busied myself with extracting bits of dead leaf from a cut on my shin. 'That's for me to know, and for you to – sssss! – find out,' I said. 'Like I told you, I'll have to connect with the ghost of John Wilkes. I've seen him already. I just need to, like, hook up with him properly. He knows what he took from Sir Ambrose, and he knows where he put it.'

'Yeah, two and a half centuries ago!' said Sam. 'And, "Hook up with him properly"? So, what, you're going to *summon* the ghost of this man that died two hundred years ago or something–'

'Right.'

'...Then you're going to somehow talk to him...even though you haven't yet *talked* to a ghost—'

'I *have*.'

'...Yeah but not so's they'd answer back. Not only that, but you're hoping he's going to reveal this information especially to you, something that's been kept secret for over two centuries, and may in any case be no use at all by now—'

'Hey, what do you care?' I snapped, chucking the used cotton wool pad. 'It's my problem, not yours!' I sure as hell wasn't going to admit he had a point.

'I'm just curious,' said Sam. 'And...look, if you're hellbent on doing this thing then man, are you gonna need help! Hey, I think you're crazy and everything, but I'll do what I can. We made a good team last time, I thought.'

I picked up another cotton pad and soaked it in acid-green antiseptic. 'Oh, is that what we are? A team? I thought you and your *Insula Club* buddies were too busy being a team.'

'Ah, Kit, come on,' said Sam. 'Don't be like that! It's just something to do, that's all. Look, I'm sorry. I'm just a bit scared for you, that's all. I want to help, really I do.'

'Well, thanks and everything, but this is *my* battle. I don't need help from any boy.' I thought for a moment. 'In fact, you know what? I'm going to make that a rule: I'm allowed to have help from other people, but only if they're girls. Don't take it personally, but boys are out.'

Sam chewed his lip. 'Fine,' he said at last, kicking a loose clod of earth. 'Don't say I didn't offer.'

'I won't.' I collected up all my dead tissues and cotton pads.

'And don't bother to come running when you get into trouble, either,' Sam added.

'Nope.'

Sam just stood and watched as I collected everything. 'I'd like to see you try to figure things out with the Giggle Sisters as your only–'

'Right, suppertime,' I announced, as I got up and headed inside.

Next morning I ached all over.

'Come on, *Kitaki-mou*, get up,' said Maro. She was holding a humungous map. 'It's a lovely day for that hike across the Chiltern Hills.'

I groaned. I knew this was the plan, but I couldn't face it. Besides, I had other things to deal with. '*How* long did you say it was?'

'Not far, only about seven miles.'

I sat up. 'Seven miles!'

'Oh Kitty, you'll love it. It's gorgeous round here.'

'Kitty, you *have* to come,' said Flossie. 'It'll be boring without you.'

I flopped back down on my pillow. 'Oh Floss, I'm sorry, but I can't go. Maro, I didn't say anything, but I had an accident yesterday. My leg still really hurts.' I rubbed it and winced, for extra effect.

'It's true,' said Sam. 'She's trying to be all brave, but she did have a pretty bad fall.'

Thank you, Sam, I thought. For a moment I felt slightly less fed up with him. It was nice of him to be supportive, even if he did think I was out of my tiny mind, and even though I'd banned him from helping out.

Maro's face crumpled with sympathy. 'Oh, *pethaki-mou*, I'm sorry – I didn't know. Is it that bad? Maybe I should take you to see a doctor–'

'No, no,' I said quickly. Better not overdo it. 'I think I just need to take it easy.'

'Maybe we should do the walk tomorrow,' suggested Flossie.

'I don't want to take the chance with the weather, *pethaki-mou*,' said Maro. 'Today is perfect. Tomorrow it looks like rain again.'

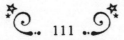

Flossie gave me a pleading look. Now that Emily was out of the picture, suddenly I was Buddy No. 1 again. 'Well, it's not like I can't walk around a *bit*,' I said. 'Maybe I should just go with you for a little while, then come back to the Hippo and hang.' *And figure out how to get to the caves*, I thought. Which I hadn't had a chance to do yet. I suspected they were still too far away to get to by bike. Hmm. Major drawback. Unless…

'Where are the Chiltern Hills, anyway?' I asked.

'The other side of the river, *pethaki-mou*. They're–' Maro was interrupted by a call on her mobile. 'Dinky! *Kalimera!*' Her cheery grin quickly disappeared though. Putting the map down on the table, she disappeared out the front door, while we gazed after her.

'I wonder what's up now,' said Sam.

'I hope Emily's OK,' said Flossie.

'Em'll be fine,' I said, just to cheer her up. She looked so worried. Though I didn't like the look of Maro's reaction either; not very encouraging. So much for things settling down again with me out of the way…

I tried to distract Floss with the map. 'Is this the route she's got worked out then?' I said. A red line had been drawn on the map, forming a sort of elongated hexagon.

'Yeah,' sighed Flossie. 'It's gonna be so boring.'

Studying the route, I noticed something. 'Hang on, is West Wycombe part of the walk?'

Sam peered at the map. 'She didn't mention it, but...yeah, looks as if it is.'

There was a blue 'P' sign close to the village – and *very* close to the Hellfire Caves, which were marked as well. My mind was ticking over. 'So you could set out from there I guess, right?'

Sam gave me a curious look. 'I *guess*...'

'OK, great!' I said. 'I'll come for part of the walk.' I could get *close* to the caves. Now all I had to figure out was how to get in. But I would work something out – I was determined. By now I'd pretty much given up on connecting with Sir Ambrose, but it certainly looked as if Wilkes was haunting the caves. I was nervous of him, but I'd have to get over that. I needed him now.

I was just starting to feel all excited when Maro came back in, her face tight with worry. 'Emily's been taken to casualty,' she said.

The words hit my gut with a thud.

Just *what* were we dealing with here?

Tunnel Vision

We went round with get well cards, DVDs and chocolates. Em was back home, but she'd had a terrible night.

'The cough got worse and triggered an asthma attack in the middle of the night,' Maro had explained. 'She's never had one before, apparently...but don't worry, she's better now.'

Dinky looked wrung out, but pleased to see us. 'Poor thing, she was practically *blue*,' she said. 'Gasping for breath. And of course we didn't have any inhalers, because none of us has ever needed them before...oh, Maro, it was terrifying!' She looked about to break down in tears. Maro comforted her.

Dinky brightened quickly. 'Anyway, go on up. All under control now. But she's very tired.'

'It's OK,' said Maro. 'We won't stay long.'

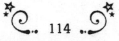

We went up to see Em, and I couldn't stop the big question going round and round in my head:

Did this happen because of the curse?

What if the thing was still getting stronger, and had nothing to do with whether I was there or not? There was no way of telling. But when I thought back to what Dinky had said about it, it did look scarily like a possibility.

Well, whether or not I could help by staying away as much as possible, I wasn't taking any chances. So when Maro offered to do some grocery shopping for Dinky, I jumped at the chance to go with her. On my way out, I peered around for signs of more destruction. Because of course the other question burning up my brain was: had there been any more things flying around in the night? I couldn't exactly ask.

All of this meant that the day was fast disappearing, and I *still* hadn't made it to the caves.

And after seeing poor, pale little Emily in her bed, dosed up with about twenty different kinds of drugs and inhalers – and what with all the blood test results they were waiting on as well – time was running out.

Because if this *was* connected to the curse, Emily might not get better at all.

What with all the errands and everything, we didn't start

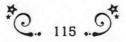

our walk until late. The good thing was, I succeeded in getting Maro to use West Wycombe as the starting point for her hike. Result! It was a brilliantly warm, sunny day. I dutifully trekked a couple of kilometres to the next village, but then I started limping, so Maro cut me some slack and let me go back to the Hippo. The downside was, she set me some homework to do once I was there.

Well, I wasn't doing it – I had to get to the caves. By the time I was heading back to West Wycombe, hot and sweaty, it was getting on for four o'clock. Finding my way back was easy. West Wycombe Hill was higher than the others around it, and easy to identify because of the huge hexagonal mausoleum at the top, and the church topped with a massive golden ball. That golden ball shone on the horizon for miles around; I didn't even need the map Maro had given me.

As it turned out, there weren't too many visitors at the caves. 'Been very slow today,' said Carol, as she cleared tables in the café courtyard. 'First really fine day of spring, last thing people want to do is disappear down a dank tunnel! How come you're back so soon, then?'

'I'm doing a project,' I said. 'We're home-schooled, you see. Only…my grandma doesn't know I'm here,' I added, following her indoors. 'It's a surprise. She told us each to pick something in the area that interests us, and do our own thing. I think she'll be really pleased when I'm done!'

'Oh great!' said Carol. 'You could do a really interesting piece about this place, all those stories about ghosts, spells, secret passages…in fact, I tell you what,' she added, diving behind the counter and bringing out a token for the turnstile. 'Have a free pass.' She looked at the clock. 'Well, I'm off in a minute, so if you've got any questions, fire away.'

'Um, you said there were secret passages?'

'Oh, well, just *stories*, love!' said Carol. 'No one's ever actually found one – though there may have been a different layout at one time.'

'OK, thanks,' I said. 'Oh, and what time do you close?'

'Five-thirty,' said Carol.

'OK, cool.' I waved the token as I made to leave. 'Thanks for this!'

Result again – a free pass! I'd scraped some coins together, but wasn't sure I had enough. Good bit of fibbing, I thought. Only it wasn't really a lie, was it? I *was* doing a project – and if I succeeded, then Maro would definitely be pleased with me. *If* I succeeded, that was…

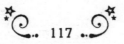

I set off. No sign of Sukie this time. I guess she might have appeared if I'd hung around that part of the caves, but I was on a mission. I had the crumpled picture of John Wilkes in my pocket – I clutched it in my hand now. It helped me to focus on him, try to connect with his spirit. Down I went. The tunnel grew cooler, and the passages between the lit displays seemed longer and darker than I remembered – probably because this time there were far fewer visitors. I shivered.

OK, John Wilkes, I'm coming to get you!

The thought of it churned my stomach. *God, Kitty, don't lose your nerve now!* I reminded myself about poor Emily in her bed…the smashed glasses and the collapsed dresser…the look of horror on Dinky's face. The fear in her voice when she'd told Maro about the curse. And I thought of poor old Sir Ambrose, a shadow of his former self, dying alone in the flaming house. And the picture in my head of that raging fire turned into the flames of the campfire and the laughing, devilish face of Little Boy Blue; finally, I thought of my anger at Louis and his gang, and my completely bonkers declaration that I was going to lift the curse.

Oh, I was coming to get Wilkes, all right; I was determined.

It was so much quieter this time, hardly anyone

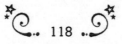

around. I passed through the Banqueting Hall into the farthest reaches of the caves. Here, the light grew dim and the music receded. All I could hear were my own footsteps echoing off the gravelly ground. I was completely alone. Finally, I crossed the 'River Styx' and came once more to the Inner Temple, and its creepy group of shop-dummies. There he sat, the Wilkes one, with his white wig, blue satin jacket and ugly frozen grin.

I stared at the dummy. 'I won't give up, you know!' I told him – then realised I'd said it aloud. Well, I didn't care any more. 'I know you're in here somewhere, you ugly devil!' I added.

There were voices in the tunnel behind me – other visitors.

I hung about, forced to listen over and over again to the recording about the baboon incident while I waited for them to leave. They were distracting; so was the recording. I wandered back up the passage...over and over in my head, I went on calling out to John Wilkes's ghost. Every now and then, I thought I caught a glimpse of him. But it was always just in the corner of my eye. As soon as I turned, he was gone. Or was I imagining it? I couldn't tell. *That devil Wilkes.* He was playing games with me, I swore he was.

Time frittered away. For another whole hour, I hung

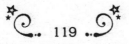

about, going back and forth over the River Styx. 'I'm not leaving until you come out, Wilkes!' I called.

'*The Hellfire Caves will be closing in twenty minutes*,' said an announcement. '*Please make your way to the exit.*'

No way! They would have to come and drag me out.

All right – come on!

I headed back towards the Inner Temple, over the River Styx. And there, silhouetted against the light, was a solitary figure, just standing there with his back to me. Wilkes! It had to be. This was no live visitor – not with that long, black cloak, white stockings and buckled shoes. No wig though; just short, dark hair. But maybe he didn't always wear it?

'Wilkes?' I called. 'Is that you?'

I stepped closer.

The figure just stood there, not moving.

'I need to talk to you,' I said. 'This is important.'

Still he didn't move. I went even closer. 'Please turn around,' I said. 'I need to see you.'

I waited, gazing at the tall, dark figure. Then all of a sudden, he turned around. Under the cloak he was wearing a white shirt. He stared straight at me, he reached up with both hands and–

'Aargh!' I cried, and fell over backwards. It was the most horrible thing I'd ever seen.

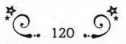

The Gold Snuffbox

The ghost stood there, looming over me. He had opened his shirt, and there, underneath, was a bloody, gaping wound. His glistening ribs had pieces missing from them, and underneath, where his heart should be, was just a black hole. He went on staring down at me with his desolate expression.

'No, no, no!' I cried, hiding my face.

Paul Whitehead. That's who it was, I realised now – the ghost who searched the caves for his missing heart. Not Wilkes. I scrambled back towards the wall and curled myself up into a ball, hoping and praying he'd go away. I must have stayed like that for several minutes. The announcement said, '*The Hellfire Caves will be closing in ten minutes. Please make your way to the exit.*'

I'm not scared, I kept saying to myself, over and over. *I'm not scared.* He wouldn't hurt me…would he? How

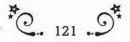

loud had I screamed? I wasn't sure. I just hoped no one had heard. I might have been drowned out by the soundtrack – I hoped so.

'Wilkes, you have to come *now,* you ugly devil!' I called, from inside the scrunched-up ball I'd made of myself. 'I can't stand this any more!'

Suddenly, the caves were plunged into silence. The soundtrack had been switched off. Any minute now, someone would come along to shoo me out of there. Then a soft, whispering voice – so soft, I could barely make it out – said, *'Oh yesss, so very ugly!'*

At last, I uncurled from my ball and looked up. Whitehead was gone – thank god – but I couldn't see anyone else. 'What did you say?'

'Ug-leee as the De-villl!' said the whispering, echoing voice.

It was coming from down the passageway, in the direction of the Inner Temple – I was sure of it. I got up and ran down there.

And there he stood, leaning against the gate, clear as day. His voice, too, was bright and clear now: 'Well, I may be ugly, but it takes me just half an hour to talk away my face!'

I stared at him. 'Oh my god, it really is you!'

What with all the waiting and waiting to see him,

plus the shake-up I'd just had over the ghost of Paul Whitehead, I thought I'd burst with relief and excitement. And this time there really was no doubt that this was Wilkes – the squint, the heavy jaw, the tombstone teeth...no one else looked like him.

But at the same time I was angry. 'Why the hell did you take so long?' I demanded.

'Are we discussing minutes or years here?' he replied coolly.

'Oh, very funny. I've been waiting...oh my god!' I'd just realised what had happened. 'You answered me! Oh, this is incredible!'

Wilkes, on the other hand, was acting like this sort of thing happened every day. 'Shall I start, then?' he asked.

'Start what?'

'The talking away my face.'

'What do you mean?'

'My famous charm, of course,' said Wilkes. 'People soon forget–'

He was interrupted by a voice from along the passageway behind me. 'Hello? Is anyone still here?'

'Oh for god's sake, this is such rubbish timing! No, don't talk,' I told Wilkes. 'No – hang on, I mean, *do*. Just–'

'We're closing up now!' called the voice from down the way.

'Yes! Just coming!' I called back, then turned to Wilkes. My heart was banging against my ribs so hard, I thought I'd faint from the stress of it all. 'OK, you!' I growled at him. 'I don't have a minute to waste here. So come on: you put a curse on Sir Ambrose Vyner, and it's still affecting his family even now, and it's got to stop, you understand? It's got to…wait! Don't go!'

But Wilkes was already fading before my eyes. 'I'm sometimes up at the mausoleum, you know,' he said, his voice reduced to a whisper again. Then he vanished altogether.

'I'm sorry, miss, but you really do have to leave now,' said the guard, who now appeared from around the bend in the tunnel.

'Yes, yes…sorry!' Trembling, I headed out.

I ran out, blinking in the daylight, and scrambled up the hill towards the mausoleum. *Oh, please let him show up!* I thought. I felt I would go crazy if I couldn't follow through now. And all the time I was thinking, *My god, he actually talked to me!* Not *at* me, but *to* me! This was incredible. I'd never spent so long trying to connect with a spirit…and I'd worked so hard at it, I thought my head would split. But it had paid off – he'd appeared, and he'd *talked* to me!

I heaved my way up the rough stone steps. Soon, the

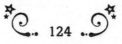

huge mausoleum loomed above me, like a stone fortress. I was almost at the top of the hill when suddenly a familiar, disgusting smell hit me, like rotten eggs. 'Urgh!' I clamped my hand to my nose. Oh, not again!

I half-expected to see Louis' mates, but then I heard a man's laughter, and a split second later, Wilkes appeared in front of me, grinning his tombstone grin. 'Good, eh?'

'You bean the sbell?' I asked, still holding my nose. 'Dat was you?'

'Hee hee! Sulphur! Good trick, eh? I've not tried that one before.'

'Oh for crying out loud.'

'Well, you asked for it,' said Wilkes. 'Calling me a devil, and all that nonsense. Thought you deserved a spot of brimstone. Hmm…still can't get the hang of the blasted vapour cloud thing though. There *wasn't* a vapour cloud, was there?'

'No.'

I took my hand off my nose and looked around, to check we were alone, then turned back to Wilkes. 'OK, don't disappear again, I need to talk to you.'

Wilkes put his head in his hands. 'I *know*,' he groaned.

'You…you know? OK, I don't really know how

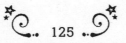

this works. How do you–'

'Women!' snapped Wilkes. 'Nag, nag, nag, all the time! You give a man earache.'

'What, you mean *I've* been nagging *you*?'

'Oh, I suppose you might call it persuading, wheedling, cajoling…no. Outright nagging. Persistent, aren't you? I couldn't even get Paul to scare you off.'

'Whitehead? You mean–'

'Thought it might do the trick,' said Wilkes. He sighed loudly. 'But no!'

I couldn't help laughing. 'Oh, but this is incredible! See, I've only just developed my phantorama, and–'

Wilkes gave a big, loud yawn, which quickly shut me up. 'Young lady, if you think I have the *slightest* interest in you, you are very much mistaken. I only came here to tell you to leave me in peace. You've had your fun and games, now kindly respect the deceased and be on your way.'

'What? Are you kidding? No way!'

Wilkes gazed at me and not at me at the same time. That squint of his was majorly unsettling. 'You really are a defiant little madam. You're not a *Scot*, are you?'

'What the hell's that got to do with anything? No, I'm not, and anyway I know some really nice Scottish people, if you must know.' Furious now, I wagged a finger at him. 'Look, Sir Ambrose's family are having

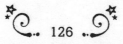

a terrible time! So whatever the hell it is you did to put this curse on him, you overdid it big time, and I need you to *un*do it, *now*.'

I was trembling, and the words were spilling out faster than I could think. 'I mean, I know you're dead and everything' – I looked away, slightly embarrassed – 'but…well, if there's anything *I* can do, seeing as I'm actually, like, *alive*…then just tell me what to do, and I'll do it! What did you steal from him – a watch? A uh, thingy – what did Dinky say? A snuffbox?'

Wilkes just stood there, frowning, stroking his chin. Then his lips parted into that garish tombstone grin. He burst out laughing. 'Oh, yes!' he said at last. 'What fun we can have with this…what fun!' He threw back his head, guffawing loudly.

'Fun?' I said. 'FUN? Do you realise how terrified that family are right now? And now they're getting sick, and–'

'Aah…all right, young lady, calm down. Must say, I am rather impressed the curse has lasted this long. Remarkable! But you're right. There's nothing I can do now…*you*, on the other hand – yes, you might.'

'What? Tell me what!'

'It's very simple,' said Wilkes. 'You're right. I did rather cheekily borrow something from Sir Ambrose –

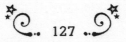

a gold snuffbox. And I –' he chuckled like a naughty schoolboy – 'I hid it. Now, all you have to do is to find the snuffbox, and return it to the family.'

'Yes! Yes! Where is it?'

'Ah, now, that's the thing,' said Wilkes. 'I'm trying to remember…'

'You don't *know?*'

'Well, it has been a while, you know! Oh, but wait…here's how it goes:

> Cross from the Abbey, upon the shore,
> Full square from the ancient tower,
> Twelve paces southward–'

'Wait, wait,' I said. 'What is this? Why don't you just tell me where it is!'

'Oh, but that wouldn't be half as much fun,' said Wilkes. And he carried on:

> 'Twelve paces southward go thee before,
> Thy prize to find beneath the bower.'

Then he began to fade.

'No! Don't go!' I begged. 'Tell me that again, this isn't fair!'

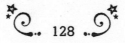

'Ah…energy going now,' said Wilkes. He repeated the verse, but his voice was fading along with his image. I had to strain to take it all in. Then as soon as he was done, he disappeared altogether.

'Wilkes? Wilkes!' I called.

But it was no use; he was gone. Leaving me with nothing but a stupid riddle to go on. How the hell was I going to figure this out?

Wild Goose Chase

'Charlie's had an accident.'

Maro had just got off the phone with Dinky and she looked worried.

'What happened?' I asked.

'He's all right. He fell down the stairs, but nothing's broken. Just has to walk with a crutch for a few days. *The-eh mou*, those poor people, so many problems!'

Yes, and we both know why, I thought.

Maro sighed. 'Well, nothing we can do...finish your breakfast, *pethakia*. There's a museum I want to take you to.'

I was prepared for this – and I would have to stall it. My hunt for buried treasure couldn't wait. 'Oh, could we just go for a quick bike ride along the riverside first?' I asked. 'It's good exercise!'

As I'd hoped, this worked. As long as Good Exercise

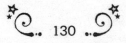

was involved, Maro was usually happy to get rid of us for an hour or two.

Once we were off the campsite, I was able to explain to the others the real reason for the excursion.

'OK, Sam, you go and see Louis or something. Flossie and I have some business to attend to.'

'We do?' said Flossie.

'Oh, I get it,' said Sam. 'This is something *boys* can't be involved in, right?'

'Right.'

He gave me that sideways look of his. 'Hang on, have you–'

'Not telling, Sam. Now scram!' To be honest, I'd have welcomed Sam's help. He's a bit of a swot, so would probably be really useful for riddle-solving…but no. I was sticking to my guns.

'Fine,' he said, mounting his bike. 'Good luck!' he yelled as he rode off. Sarcastic.

Flossie looked completely confused. 'What's going on?'

'Floss, this is top secret. You mustn't say anything, even to Emily. OK?'

'OK.'

I told her all about Sir Ambrose's snuffbox, and the curse put on him by Wilkes. But I regretted it as soon as

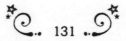

I got to the part about Emily.

Flossie looked panicked. 'Oh my god! You mean, her life's in danger?'

'No, no,' I said quickly – though to be honest, I couldn't know that for sure. 'The curse is too old, it's not strong enough for that,' I lied. 'But it's having a terrible effect on the whole family, and the sooner we fix it, the better.'

The idea had lodged itself in Flossie's brain though, and it wasn't going anywhere. 'We've got to save her life!' she cried. 'There isn't a minute to lose! What do we have to do?'

I explained how I'd managed to communicate with the ghost of John Wilkes, and that he'd given me a clue to where the snuffbox was hidden. I pulled a piece of paper from my pocket where I'd scrawled what I could remember of the riddle, and showed it to her:

Across from the Abbey, on the shore,
??? the ancient tower
Go twelve paces southwards
And find your prize...the bower

Flossie frowned. 'Huh?'

'I know,' I said. 'I didn't have anything to write with

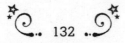

at the time. This was all I could remember. I think I might have figured it out, though. OK, so the "Abbey"…remember there's that place along the river that Maro pointed out?'

'The one with the ruined tower?'

'That's the one. It *has* to be that place he's talking about. I mean, how many abbeys can there be on the river right around here?'

Flossie shrugged.

'There's that bunch of question marks – he said something about squares, don't remember now…and that word "bower". I didn't know what it meant, so I looked it up. It means a shady place in a garden. So here's what I think the whole thing probably means: the snuffbox is buried in a shady place, twelve paces from the riverbank, directly opposite the ruined tower of the Abbey.'

'Are you sure?' asked Flossie.

'Not a hundred per cent, no. But it's worth giving it a shot.'

'How are we going to dig it up?'

'Oh, I thought of that.' I reached into the knapsack on my bike and pulled out a trowel and a gardening fork. 'They're Charlie's,' I explained. 'I borrowed them when we went round last night…er, not that he knows about it.'

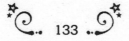

'Well, at least he won't be using them today, not with that injury of his,' Flossie pointed out.

'That's true. And when I let him have them back, we'll also be able to present them with the little golden snuffbox!'

'And tell them that *a-a-a-ll* their troubles are over!' said Flossie.

'OK, Floss, let's not get too carried away. But yeah, that's about the size of it. Only we don't *say* anything about the curse, OK? Dinky knows, and Louis knows…I reckon Charlie does too. The only one who doesn't is Emily – which is just as well. And they don't know that *we* know. All right, come on, let's go.'

We cycled as far as we could until the path got all overgrown, so we hid our bikes in the shrubbery and trudged the rest of the way on foot. Soon we were back out in the open and the river and the fields and the whole caboodle were visible again. Only, no Abbey.

'The river bends around, don't you remember?' said Flossie. 'If we keep going, maybe it'll appear.'

So on we went, through more trees, out the other side…and there it was: the old tower. We ran on, splashing through puddles, dodging nettles… I pictured the look on Louis' face when he saw the golden box…oh, yes! What a delicious moment that was going

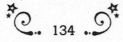

134

to be. I even – I couldn't help it – imagined Emily leaping miraculously from her bed, all rosy-cheeked and bathed in golden light, accompanied by a chorus of angels. Yeah, daft, I know, but let me tell you the anticipation was *killing* me.

The trouble with wanting something *really badly*, is you get scared that somehow you'll never have it.

And that's what happened.

I slowed down, panting. 'Oh, Flossie!' I gasped.

'What?'

'The snuffbox! It's made of *gold*. Or at least gold plate.'

'Ye-es…'

'And it was buried two hundred and fifty-odd years ago!'

'And…?'

'Well, think about it! What are the chances it's still there? People might have been round here with metal detectors. It could've been discovered and taken away, and put in a museum or something!'

'Oh,' said Flossie. 'That wouldn't be great.'

'Oh, Floss!' I wiped my hot, sweaty face on my sleeve. As if in sympathy, the clouds gathered overhead, and the sky grew dark.

'Well, we don't know that's happened,' Flossie pointed out. 'It might still be there.'

'Yes…yes,' I nodded. 'Of course. Not saying we shouldn't *look*. Just that…oh, god. Come on.'

In no time we were standing in the spot directly opposite the ruined tower. 'OK, twelve paces from here.'

Flossie strode forward, then stopped. 'How big are the paces meant to be?'

'Well, adult size,' I said. '*Male* adult size. Like….this.' I strode forward, like I was stepping over a boulder or something. Then another boulder, and another one… 'Oh,' I said, as I realised I was about to collide with a tree. 'That probably wasn't there two hundred and fifty years ago.'

'You'll just have to go round it,' said Flossie.

'Yeah…and fast-forward a couple of paces, I guess. So here, that would be pace number *nine*. Ten…eleven… twelve.' I stopped. 'Well, could be worse, might've been a tree grown right in the spot where we're meant to dig.' I kicked away the dead leaves, bringing out a musty smell and worms and centipedes. 'OK, here goes.' I kneeled down and stabbed at the ground with the trowel. It was like trying to cut stale bread with a butter knife. I stabbed some more. Gradually, the earth began to break up a little.

Flossie hacked with the gardening fork, which was even more rubbish. 'If only we had a spade!'

We hacked and we hacked and slowly the earth

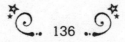

broke up and our hole got wider and deeper. I sat back on my heels, puffing. 'Flossie?' I said.

'Yeah?'

'Do you feel ever-so-slightly completely insane, doing this?'

'Oh, don't give up, Kit!' said Flossie, her face now bright red as she went on digging. 'It's got to be around here some– Hang on, I think I hit something.'

'You did?'

Flossie reached down into the hole and pulled away the clumps of earth. 'It doesn't really seem box-shaped, more sort of…curvy.'

I worked quickly with the trowel, scraping away around the edges of the thing. 'Oh,' I sighed. 'That's 'cause it's just a root.'

'No, wait,' said Flossie. 'Underneath, look. There's a corner.'

'Oh wow, you're right!'

We dug and scraped like mad, reaching awkwardly down underneath the root. As more of the box appeared, we found the lower edge of it and dug under that.

'It's awfully dark, for something that's made of gold,' said Flossie.

'Yeah, well, it's covered in dirt, though, isn't it,' I said. 'Although…hmm. It doesn't even look like *dirty* gold.

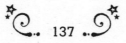

Looks more like…wood.'

'Seems big, too,' said Flossie. 'Didn't you say it was something he carried around in his pocket?'

'Yeah…hey, maybe the snuffbox is inside! That's it – it *has* to be. This thing is buried right where Wilkes said the snuffbox would be. That has to mean something.'

I pawed away, my fingernails jammed full of dirt…the anticipation was killing me. Finally the earth crumbled away underneath the box. I yanked on it, and at last I had it in my hands.

The box was about the size of a chunky book. It was made of dark wood, its lid inlaid with a beautiful rose design. Pulse racing, I opened it up – and immediately, my heart sank. 'Oh.'

No snuffbox.

Instead, lying on red silk lining, was an old envelope, sealed with red sealing wax. Fingers trembling, I broke it open; inside was a really old-looking iron key, and a piece of paper. On it was a handwritten note:

To Whom It May Concern

Alas thou hast not yet done enough
To locate th'elusive Box of Snuff!

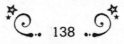

Didst thou honestly believe 'twould be,
That Mister Wilkes might give it to thee,

With nary a trick, nor a riddle?
Then, Sir, thine head is ful of piffle!

Two more tasks I set thee now…

There was more, but I couldn't go on.

'Two more tasks! I could strangle him!'

'If he was alive,' said Flossie.

'Well, obviously.'

We stood there in silence as I gazed at the note, trying to make sense of it.

'Which he isn't,' added Flossie.

'I *know*.'

Two more tasks…I was being sent on a wild goose chase!

'I mean, if someone's already dead, then it would be hard to–'

'Flossie! I *know*.' I heaved a massive sigh. I held up the key, a heavy thing, about the size of a wax crayon. 'God,' I said. 'How are we ever going to make sense of this?'

Echoing around the glade, I swore I could hear wicked, taunting laughter.

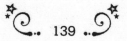

A Riddle

I had a key. But a key to what? And two more tasks to perform.

But at the moment, all we had were 'instructions' – if you could call them that – for one of them. The rest of the message went on:

My first is in France but 'tis not in Bordeaux;
My second in Norway, but not in Oslo.

My last is in New Hampshire, but not in Maine;
They wore me in Phrygia, come sun or rain.

My mark in the caves is the sign for you;
From thence go you paces twenty and two.

Then take the pick and find the stile
Where once I did my love beguile.

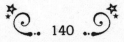

'Lemme see!' demanded Flossie.

I showed it to her.

'*What?*' she said. 'I don't get any of this! Only…this mark in the "caves"; is that the Hellfire Caves, then?'

'I guess…' I read the riddle again and again, but every time I did I just got into more of a panic. 'But all this stuff about things in France and not in Bordeaux and stuff… How the hell would I know?'

'Well…we've got to go back now,' said Flossie. 'How you gonna get to the caves again?'

'No idea. But if I go AWOL for a bit, you have to cover for me, Floss, understand? Just make stuff up. I don't care what you say, as long as no one comes looking for me.'

'Oh, Kitty…I'm all worried now!'

'Well, don't be,' I told her, as I stuffed the note in my back pocket. 'I'll be fine. Come on, let's go.'

'Don't worry, *agapi-mou*, no rush…we'll wait,' said Maro, talking on her mobile as we walked over to Dinky's house. As the Hippo was all hooked up at the campsite, we were borrowing Dinky's beat-up old doggy-smelly car to go to the museum. 'Dinky's been delayed,' Maro explained. She'd had to take Louis to a friend's birthday outing several miles away, and got stuck in traffic.

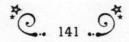

'She says we can wait at the house. Charlie'll let us in. He's working from home so as to be with Emily, and not have to travel with that leg of his. Dinky'll only be a few minutes.'

Without Louis to hang out with, Sam was dangling inconveniently. He followed me into the garden, where I'd taken myself to get away from the weird atmosphere that clung to the house, and to try and make sense of the riddle. I sat huddled over it on a bench by the rosebushes, but he wasn't deterred.

'What you got there, Kit?'

'It's a message,' I said. 'Clues, to help me find… something.'

'Oh! Not the thing that was stolen from Sir Ambrose?'

'Uh-huh,' I said, as I tried to concentrate, chewing on the end of my pen.

He peered over my shoulder. 'Let's have a look. Oh, cool! Where'd this come from?'

I snatched it away. 'Never you mind. And no help from boys, remember?'

'Ah, Kit…'

'Sorry, that's the deal. Go on, out of here.'

'Tuh! Fine, whatever,' said Sam. He mooched off and started kicking the football around.

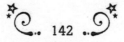

'Em's sleeping,' said Flossie, as she came over with Hetty. 'Charlie's up there with his work.'

'Oh, right…Floss? Who d'you s'pose Wilkes wrote this for?'

'Well, Sir Ambrose, right?'

'I don't think so, you know. Or if he did, it certainly wouldn't have been at the time of the curse, or what would have been the point?'

Hetty started sniffing around the note. 'No, Het,' I said, pulling it away.

'Hey, no reason the *dog* can't help,' called Sam. 'She's female, after all. Don't be so canine-ist.'

'Shut up, Sam.'

'Maybe Wilkes eventually felt bad about the whole thing,' said Flossie. 'So he thought he'd help Ambrose out.'

'Never mind that. Wouldn't it have been really risky for him to do this?' I said. 'What if he got found out? He was a really important person, don't forget – an MP and everything. I mean, I know it's *really* easy to forget that…'

'Yeah,' said Flossie.

'So like, imagine if it had got out that he was dabbling in black magic. He'd have been ruined. Mind you…look at the handwriting: kind of shaky, don't you think? Maybe he wrote it when he was old and dying.'

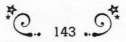

'So I guess by then he had nothing to lose,' said Flossie.

'Uh-huh.'

I read the message again. '"*My first is in France, but 'tis not in Bordeaux…*" Wait a minute, I remember now! I've seen riddles like this before. All you have to do is find a *letter* in the word "France" but not in the word "Bordeaux"! And the same with "Norway" and "New Hampshire"… The letters will spell out another word. Yay, that's it!'

'I could've told you that,' said Sam, looking over my shoulder again.

'Yeah, but you *didn't*,' I said. 'I figured it out for myself, so there.'

'Actually, you haven't figured out anything yet,' he said.

I stood up. 'Come on, Floss, let's go inside.'

Back in the weird atmosphere, I nearly tripped over an overflowing laundry basket just plonked right in the middle of the hallway. I ignored the heaviness pressing in on me in the living room – was it *worse* here? – and began crossing off letters. When I was done, we were left with:

FNC   NRWAY   WHPSR

'OK: that narrows it down a bit.'

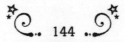

I made a list of three-letter words made up of one letter from each of these, in that order. I ignored the consonants from the middle column as they didn't make up any real words. So the list looked like this:

FAW   NAW   CAW
FAH   NAH   CAH
FAP   NAP   CAP
FAS   NAS   CAS
FAR   NAR   CAR

Plenty of which weren't words either, of course. I crossed all of those out, and was left with NAP, CAP, FAR and CAR.

'OK, so the next bit is "They wore me in…Prie-gia?" No, Friggia? I don't know how you pronounce that. "They wore me in Friggia, come sun or rain"…OK, so it must be 'CAP', that's the only one you can wear. We're getting there! Never let it be said that I can't out-swot my swotty brother.'

'Yay! But what's this "Friggia" place?' said Flossie.

I sighed. 'No idea. And what's this cap thing meant to mean?' I stood up and called out. 'Come on, wherever you are! You showed me that picture. Help me again!'

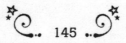 145

The door opened. Maro. 'OK, *pethakia*, Dinky's back. Time to go.'

I quickly hid the note. 'Oh, can we just quickly look something up on the computer?'

'Later, sweetie. Come on, we've got to go.'

'OK, well, where's Friggia?'

'Persia?'

'No, *Friggia.*'

'I don't know. Come on…Sam!'

I stood up, and suddenly felt really dizzy. I wobbled. 'Oh my god!'

'Kitty, are you OK?' said Flossie.

'I…yeah, I think so. Just…hey, I'm going to the loo, OK? See you out there.'

I shut myself in the downstairs loo and kneeled on the floor, not sure if I was going to throw up or not. I heard the others go out, the crunch of their feet on the drive, their muted voices…then some movement, right outside the loo door.

'Sam, is that you?'

No reply.

'Uh…Maro?'

My voice echoed off the shiny surfaces.

I shifted to the door and looked through the keyhole. No one seemed to be there.

I put the loo seat down, sat, and waited. Soon I realised I wasn't nauseous any more. Coming out, I saw that the laundry basket had been knocked over, and its contents spilled across the floor. An accident? Or the poltergeist?

Passing the living room, I couldn't resist nipping in to see if I could quickly look up "Phrygia" in a dictionary or something, then right away, my eye was drawn to the bronze statue by the couch.

Because there, perched on its head, was a red sock.

Signs

We headed out in Dinky's beat-up old doggy-smelly car.

I sat in silence, thinking. I was still a bit stunned. Sir Ambrose had answered my call! There seemed no other possible explanation. Of course I was grateful, but at the same time, frustrated. Why didn't he just *show up* and *talk to me*? But maybe he couldn't. Maybe it was all down to those evil spirits brought on by the curse. *They* were the powerful ones, and he, poor thing, was like their prisoner, shoving notes through the bars whenever he could.

I got out the note again. Never mind Phrygia, or whatever…maybe all I needed to know about the 'mark in the caves' that I had to look for was that it involved some sort of cap – possibly a red one.

'From thence go you paces twenty and two' – twenty-two! 'XXII' was the Roman numeral carving I'd seen the

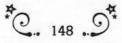

first time I'd gone to the caves. And that, I remembered, was rumoured to mark the entrance to a secret passage. But…no mention of that in the verse.

And the last part was a mystery: '*Then take the pick and find the stile, where once I did my love beguile.*' Take the pick? What did that mean? Could Wilkes be talking about the key that came with the note? Was 'pick' some oldee-fashionedee word for key? Or did he mean pick a lock? No, the wording was all wrong. Plus, you wouldn't need to pick a lock if you had a key. Hmm. As for the 'stile', I was sure there were no steps going over walls or fences anywhere in the caves, so I didn't really get that either. 'Beguile'… I had a vague idea what that meant. Sort of charm, I thought. Well something to do with love, anyway…it probably wasn't important. The red cap, the twenty-two steps and the stile – those were the things I had to go on.

By two o'clock, I was outside the Hellfire Caves once again.

I'd whizzed round the museum, done everything I was supposed to do…then I was free to go for a 'wander in the town' for an hour. Half of which was gone already, what with finding the right bus and everything.

There was nothing for it – I would have to call Sam.

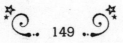

'I need more time,' I told him. 'Get Maro to stay longer, can you? I don't care what you tell her. Just... help me out here. Please?'

I could hear a sigh at the other end. 'All right. Just...don't go doing anything dangerous, OK?'

Ah. My bro – he cared. 'I won't.'

Next problem was, no Carol. So no free pass; I managed to sneak in behind some others. Yes, I knew it was wrong, but I'd make it up to whoever later. Right now, I was on a mission.

Entering the caves again made me feel a whole mish-mash of emotions: utter dread at the thought of seeing the Paul Whitehead ghost again, mixed with the pure thrill of feeling that at last I really was onto something. As for Wilkes – well, something told me I wasn't going to see his ghost here today. He wasn't going to offer any help.

There was a lot of tunnel to get through. I was worried that searching for the carving might take hours. But then, hurrying past Paul Whitehead's cave, I did a double take. There was a carving I hadn't noticed before. I went back and took a closer look. There it was, staring right back at me – a blobby, ghostly head, deeply carved, with a tall, pointed hat that clearly at one time had been painted red, though now it was quite heavily worn away.

This had to be it.

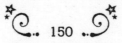

How had I missed it last time? Well, for one thing, I'd probably been too busy trying to connect with ghosts – and for another, it was situated right next to a spotlit map of the caves. *That* was the thing you noticed.

The carving was at the point where the tunnel divided in two – next to the right-hand one. '*My mark in the caves is the sign for you*'... OK, I guessed that meant I was to take *that* tunnel, rather than the one on the left. So I headed down the narrow passageway, counting the same man-sized paces as last time. It was a steep and sharply curved descent, gloomily lit with a greenish light. I got some funny looks. I didn't care.

After twenty-two paces, I stopped. There was nothing there that I could see. I went back to the carving, and started again. Again, nothing. Just dank, craggy walls. '*Find the stile, where once I did my love beguile*'. Stile, stile...there had to be *something* around here.

Then I looked up.

In the ceiling I saw a hole, covered with an iron grille. Well, it was a *thing*. But it wasn't a stile. Great. Even supposing it was possible to get up there, did I really think that the space above it would lead me to some secret passage, and there I'd find this stile? What then? I'd just go back to the entrance and ask for a ladder, right? Piece of cake!

As if…

Other people passed me as I stood there.. I didn't have a clue what to do. But the thought of giving up… *No*. I couldn't!

I eyeballed the green-lit space around it. The grille was well over two metres from the ground, and tucked away into an alcove. The wall beside it was really quite craggy – an agile person could shimmy their way up there. I supposed I was a *bit* agile; I'd certainly had some practice lately. But that wasn't the real problem. The real problem was, *no way* was I going to be able to do this without seriously attracting attention and no doubt getting dragged off to the nearest police station. What if I hid in the caves overnight, and *then* did it? OK, now I was losing it. That was clearly insane.

The tunnel went round in a semicircle, at the end of which it joined up with the other one, and the main passageway. I wandered round and round the circle, puzzling over it and fidgeting with the bag of sweets in my pocket. A bag of sweets. Where did I get them from? I took them out of my pocket. Then I realized. It wasn't sweets at all – it was the packet of stink bombs Sam had given me.

And that gave me an idea…

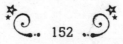

The Secret Passage

Three stink bombs. Of course! I'd forgotten all about them.

Maybe *this* was all I needed to clear the tunnel for a few minutes. After all, it was narrow and bendy here. You wouldn't see me unless you were, like, practically on top of me. I just needed to keep my little bit of tunnel clear – those stink bombs would surely do that. And the beauty of it was that 'my' bit of tunnel was avoidable. Another identical tunnel led to the same place, so why would you go down the smelly one? You wouldn't.

The downside? *I* would have to do the whole thing while gagging on the smell. Ah well…

Now I was pumped up, ready for anything. Some people came by…I waited. Then I took a stink-bomb phial and threw it down. *Aagh!* The stink was almost

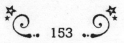

immediate, and it was *awful*. I wished I had a clothes peg for my nose.

Struggling to see as my eyes started to water from the awful fumes, I did my best to clamber up the jagged wall. I hoicked myself up, but it was *really* hard and I slipped again and again. I thought I was going to *faint* from the smell. I was leaking with sweat and my chest wanted to explode. I heard some hollow gasps down the way – the evil stink-fug was spreading.

OK, this time I was going to do it. I couldn't fail. Right foot, left foot, right hand, left hand. Cold, clammy, crags. Inch by inch. Muscles screaming with the strain, but keeping on…up and up…

Now I was hunched in the curve, the rusty iron grille *just* within reach… I felt around, searching for a keyhole, but couldn't find one. I edged higher. Now I could grab the wooden ledge supporting the grille…but I needed more time. I took out another stink phial and dropped it. More stink-fug. *Urghh*…

Would the grille just push open? I tried…and yes! It lifted up.

'Eurgh, what's that smell?' came a voice from down the way.

Reaching up, I got a grip on the wooden ledge and I hoisted myself up.

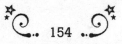

'I wouldn't go down there. It stinks!' said someone else.

Now the job was easier. I had a solid ledge to lever myself up on, and in seconds I was up inside the dark space, banging my head on another roof above me. I put the grille back in place, sat down and heaved a sigh of relief. I'd done it. Well, part of it, anyway. But what was the key for?

I looked around, but there wasn't much to see. The only light came from the grille, and that was pretty dim. I wished I'd thought to bring a torch, but everything had happened so quickly, I hadn't had a chance to think things through. All I could do was feel around, using the tiny rectangle of light from my phone to help me see. I soon discovered that the space was enclosed on three sides; the fourth was mostly pitch black. I felt my way round to it; there was a hole there. I got down onto my front and edged through on my elbows and knees – it wasn't deep enough for me to crawl. I put my hand out into the darkness ahead of me, holding my phone. The tunnel went on. At first I could still hear the echoing cheesy music from the Hellfire Caves voice-over; then it grew fainter, and died.

Then the ground ahead of me fell away. My heart lurched. The darkness was starting to do my head in

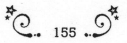

now: the phone could light up only a tiny patch of wall or floor, if I held it close – otherwise it was useless. But I could see that I'd come to a ledge. What lay beyond it? I had to find out – even though my imagination was running wild. The clammy stillness was closing in on me. Trembling, I held out my phone, and could dimly make out another ledge immediately below it. Steps? Could this be the stile, or part of it? I shifted around so my legs were in front of me, and felt ahead with my feet. One step…two…three…yes! They kept on going! Down with the feet, shift-bumping on my bum.

I thought I heard whispering voices ahead of me…or were they behind me, back in the caves? I couldn't tell.

Finally, I hit solid ground. Now I could stand up. My little rectangle of light told me there was a chalk wall either side of me. I'd come back down to about the same level as the caves, in what seemed like a normal, human-scale tunnel. I leaned my back against the wall, consumed in the blackness.

There was no air in here.

There was no nothing.

I wanted to go back.

But there was still the key…I pulled it from my pocket and turned it over in my hand. What was it for? I had to find out. I couldn't turn back, not now. And the

whispers…there they were again. I jumped. A face was hovering like a misty moon in front of me. It was Suki, the jilted bride, with her sickly grin. The whispers sharpened, like a blurry picture coming into focus: 'He'll be along directly. I know he will!'

It took me a second to collect myself. '"*Find the stile, where once I did my love beguile*",' I recited to her, at last. Was she the 'love' spoken of in the verse? 'Where is the stile, Sukie?' I asked.

She just went on grinning blankly. 'He's been delayed, is all,' she said. 'Any minute now…'

'He went that way,' said another voice, and Wilkes suddenly emerged from the gloom. He pointed to the steps, and Sukie sailed over and dissolved into them. I looked away – I didn't want to see the bloody mess at the back of her head again.

I was so relieved to see Wilkes, I actually forgot to find anything freaky-outish about the situation. 'Wilkes! Am I here? Is this the place?'

He nodded. 'Yes, this is the place. Well done, well done. Not a *stile* in the truest sense, but, you know, steps leading to the top of a wall…ah well, the chap wasn't the greatest poet, after all.'

'"The chap"? I thought you were talking about *your* love?'

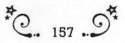

'Oh no, I just stole that part,' said Wilkes. He shook his head. 'Tut-tut-tut, poor little Sukie. I've tried telling her, but she won't listen. Typical woman.'

Don't let him wind you up, I told myself, *you need something from him.* I ignored his remark and asked, 'Well, what did "take a pick" mean?'

'As in "take *your* pick",' explained Wilkes. 'As in, choose which passage.'

'Ah. And the key…' I held it up. 'What's it for?'

'Oh, the key!' said Wilkes. 'Ah yes, I almost forgot. It's been a while, you know…how long *has* it been, anyway? Fifty years? A hundred?'

'More like two hundred and thirty!' I told him. 'Or maybe less. I don't actually know when you died.'

Wilkes gave a low whistle. 'Impressive, even if I say so myself. Just shows how belligerent you females can be, disturbing my rest after all this time. Are you *sure* you're not a Scot?'

Ignore it! 'We were talking about the *key*, Mr Wilkes,' I said through gritted teeth, wagging it under his nose.

'Yes, yes, the key…the key!' he repeated teasingly. 'You want to unlock the secret, but there's just one problem – you have the key in your hand, but you don't know what it's *for*. Story of your life, I expect…am I right?' He gave me a knowing wink.

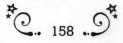

God, he was annoying! 'I don't know what you're talking about,' I snapped. 'Just...can you *please* tell me what I'm meant to do with this thing. I haven't got much time. The curse is growing stronger and stronger.'

'Really?' said Wilkes, squinting at me in that unnerving way of his. 'Extraordinary. Well, I should warn you, you may get more than you bargained for, young lady.' He moved closer, his ugly jaw jutting forward. 'Aren't you *afraid*?'

I leaned my head back. 'No.'

'Hmm...very well. You're only going to nag me to hell and back if we don't see this through. But don't say I didn't warn you!' He wagged a finger at me. 'The key is not for anything here in the caves, but elsewhere...for your final task.'

I shoved the key back in my pocket. 'Oh, right.' My heart sank. I'd forgotten I still had another task to do.

Wilkes began to fade. 'You need to shine your little torch right...there.' he said, pointing to the wall close to the steps.

I did so, and now I saw a carving of a large key, and the words: THE KEY TO THE VINE-CLAD TOMB. 'OK, but where–'

But Wilkes was gone now – leaving me in the dark, in more ways than one.

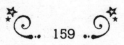

Hall of Mirrors

'How did you get all the way over here?' screeched Maro, as we hurtled down the road in the car.

'I'm sorry, I got a bit lost,' I said.

'A bit lost? Kitty, you're all the way out of town!' Then her voice softened. 'Is this anything to do with ghosts, *pethaki-mou*...your phantorama? Did something bad happen?'

'No, really, I just got confused.'

'Because you would tell me if it was, right?'

'Yes, yes,' I lied. 'I'm sorry.'

She'd picked me up somewhere between West Wycombe and the main town. I'd *tried* to walk all the way back, but I was already horribly late. So in the end I'd had to give up and answer that latest of a gazillion messages I'd had from Maro while I'd been underground without any signal on my phone.

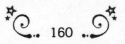

At least I was out of the caves. And that was a close call. I'd used up my last stink bomb to get out – threw it down, then jumped. Hadn't even got to my feet before some big burly security dude with his arms folded loomed over me, all lit up in the garish green light so he looked like that giant on the sweetcorn tins, only not friendly and jolly like him.

'What's going on here?' he asked.

'Nothing,' I said, and green light or not, I must've been so blatantly red-faced. 'I just fell over.'

He reached down and picked at the smashed remains of the stink-bomb phials. 'And what's all this?'

I shrugged. 'Nothing to do with me.' I brushed myself down. 'Well, bye.'

And I'd headed off down the tunnel. I never did manage to close the grille behind me. I was lucky the non-jolly green giant didn't spot that – or at least, not until I was well away.

'OK, Kitty,' said Maro now. 'Tomorrow you just have to make up the time with study at home. You don't get to come out with us.'

'OK…sorry.' *Sorry, sorry…*

'And I will be setting you plenty of work, *pethaki-mou*, and I will need to see it done. If it isn't? One more study day.'

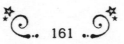

Great. That's the thing with Maro: she doesn't exactly tell you off – well, not unless she's having an off day – she's just really good at making you feel completely rubbish about what you've done. So: a whole day of no exploring. More time lost. And where the hell was this vine-clad tomb, anyway? It was probably at that big mausoleum on top of the hill back in West Wycombe. I remembered Wilkes's words, 'I'm sometimes up at the mausoleum'…and then I'd found him near there. Well, if it was, I'd probably lost out on my one and only chance to go there now that I'd upset Maro.

After all the thrills and spills of the Hellfire Caves, pretty soon I was totally wiped. We went back to the Hippo, and after dinner I fell asleep watching TV.

I was dead to the world until Maro woke me up next morning, loaded me with work, then went off for the day with Sam and Floss.

I was alone in the Hippo, staring at a pile of papers.

I *could* just sneak out for a bit, couldn't I?

But then, where would I go? I didn't *know* this 'vine-clad tomb' was at the big mausoleum. I was only guessing. Why the hell couldn't Wilkes give me straightforward instructions, just for once? Why did everything have to be a riddle? I scrawled the words all over the page:

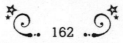

the vine-clad tomb
THE VINE-CLAD TOMB. The vine-clad tomb...

And that's when it struck me:

VINE VYNER Sir Ambrose Vyner

Was it Sir Ambrose's tomb?

The more I thought about it, the more I thought, yes…it had to be. All I had to do was find out where Sir Ambrose was buried! And pray it was nearby. But it had to be, didn't it? Well, I couldn't check. The only way to do that would be to ask Dinky, and not only didn't I have her number, but it would be just plain weird to do that out of the blue. So I would cycle to Oxenden, go to the churchyard and take a look for myself. It needn't take too long, I reckoned: I would still get the homework done. I'd just do it really fast…

I slipped on my shoes and hoody, then remembered I had to get the key out of the shorts I'd been wearing the day before. I reached into the pocket…

The key was gone.

I tried not to fly into a panic. It had probably just fallen out of my pocket onto the bed, or the floor… My bed had been flipped closed. I opened it up and felt all around the bedding, under the bed, behind it…nothing. Next I hunted all over the Hippo, every square

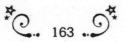

centimetre. I went through Sam's bed, and Flossie's...
I moved all their junk about. I looked in the kitchen, in
every cupboard, every nook and cranny...nothing.

Oh God, I thought. What if it had fallen out of my
pocket when I'd jumped back down from the secret
passage at the caves? No, I'd checked I still had it straight
after that, I was sure. But I still had that lurching feeling
in my gut: *it might have fallen out somewhere else in the
caves.* Or maybe in the car. Yes! Oh, please let it be there!
I seriously doubted anyone would find it there – that car
was so messy and full of junk.

But Maro was out in it again. For now, there was
nothing I could do. I didn't dare think what I would do
if it wasn't in the car – that was my only hope...

I'd just have to get on with the work she'd set me.

Close to lunchtime, I was staring at this piece I was
trying to write about bentwood chairs (this was the sort
of scintillating stuff we'd learned about at the museum
yesterday) and the words were swimming in front of
my eyes...

*The skies darkened outside, and a terrible storm came. The
Hippo shuddered...cupboards opened and slammed shut,
bang bang bang...the shower cubicle too: swish swish
swish...*

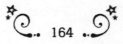

Hetty was there, barking. I held her close. 'It's OK, Hetty, don't worry.' Lights flashed on and off... Then Sukie appeared, grinning her rotten-toothed grin. 'It's right around here,' she said. 'I know it is!' And then there next to her was the ghost of Paul Whitehead, holding open his shirt. Sukie reached into the black hole where his heart should be... 'Perhaps it's in here...'

'NO, NO!' I tried to shout, but the words wouldn't come...

'Aagh!' I jolted awake so violently, the chair tipped over and I fell on the floor.

Then I realised someone was hammering on the door. I froze, staring at it.

Another knock. 'Oi! Kitty, open up! It's me, Sam.'

I leaped up. 'Sam!' I'd never been so happy to hear his voice. I went and unlocked the door.

Louis was with him.

Infuriatingly, my stupid face went all hot. Apparently it didn't know how to receive instructions like 'be cool', and had to go and turn into a beetroot. 'Oh, hi,' I said. I caught sight of my reflection in the window. I also had a huge crease down my cheek where I'd fallen asleep on my pen. *Oh, great.* I rubbed at it.

'I've been texting and calling you,' said Sam.

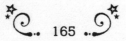

'Have you?'

'Yeah. We're going to the fair. You wanna come? Maro gave me money.'

'She did?'

'Yeah. She said you'd been on your own long enough. She's looking after Emily as Charlie had to go out.'

'Oh…' I looked at Louis. 'How is Emily?'

Louis looked away.

'She's got pneumonia,' said Sam.

'Oh my god.'

'They might have to cancel their holiday–'

'I don't care about that,' Louis butted in. 'I just want her to get better.'

'Yeah, of course, mate,' said Sam. 'Anyway, it's not contagious, so she can have visitors now, as long as they don't wear her out.'

'Oh good…I mean, good about her having visitors, that is,' I stumbled. 'Not about having pneumonia. That's awful…' *Shut up, Kitty.* I couldn't seem to think of the right thing to say. I suppose I was dealing with the unfamiliar sensation of actual sympathy towards Louis. *No!* I told myself. Remember how vile he is! *OK, but his family is cursed…* 'I'm…still working on it, you know,' I said.

'What?'

'Lifting the curse.'

'Oh…*right*,' said Louis. *And pigs might fly*, he didn't say, but he might just as well have.

'I will do it,' I told him. 'Just…had a bit of a setback, that's all.' There was an awkward silence. 'Oh, by the way,' I added. 'Your ancestor, Sir Ambrose. Where's he buried?'

'In the village,' said Louis. 'St Mary's Church. Why?'

'Oh, just wondered.' Fat lot of use that piece of information was to me if I didn't have the key, though. A heavy feeling descended on me again. Maybe the car… 'Could we just swing by your house first? There's something I think I lost in the car.'

'It's not there,' said Louis. 'It's at the garage. Got a flat tyre.'

'Oh.'

A flat tyre… How many more things were going to go wrong here? Was this yet another piece of grief caused by the curse? It felt as if everything was spinning out of control. What would it be next…Dinky losing her job? Louis drowning in a freak boating accident? I *needed* that key…

'What did you lose, Kit?' asked Sam.

'Oh, just…a worksheet. It's OK, I'll get it later.'

Louis was kind of moody all the way to the fair, but

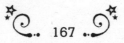

then it was like he forgot all his troubles and went totally hyper. By the time we got to the dodgems, I remembered to be cross with him. We had one car each, and he singled me out for repeated rammings, which stopped being amusing after about the third time. Worse, I never quite managed to get back at him, 'cause he was ridiculously quick at getting out of the way.

And I'd probably have done a lot better if it hadn't been for the dodgems ghost getting in the way the whole time. Mad, he was, like a crazed monkey in a cage – chewing his gum and slicking back his hair as he leaped from pole to pole, long jacket flapping. He kept popping up in front of me, which made me swerve out of the way, even though I knew there was no point.

'Never mind, eh?' said Louis, as we stepped down from the platform. 'Better luck next time!'

It's not because I'm a pathetic girl, it's because of my phantorama! I wanted to say. *You try driving one of those things with a lunatic ghost leaping in front of you every other minute!* But I didn't. I felt like leaving, but then I thought of being lonely in the Hippo, and didn't fancy that much either. So I stuck around.

Next was the Hall of Mirrors, which was a major relief after the dodgems. I hadn't been in one for *ages*. One minute we were great fat lumps with pinheads, the

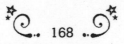

next we were dwarves with swollen heads and gigantic eyes. It had me in hysterics. Probably more than strictly necessary, to be honest. I guessed I must've been seriously tense before.

Then a figure appeared behind me. Another huge-headed dwarf – only this one was even grosser than the rest – and horribly familiar. Massive eyes turned inward, and a jutting tombstone grin – Wilkes.

I stared at him with my ridiculous big blobby eyes. 'Wilkes! What the…hey, tell me where the hell this vine-clad tomb is!' Nobody heard me amongst all the giggles.

'Oh, you can work that out,' said the ludicrous Wilkes-dwarf, moving his head in such a way now as to make his ugly mouth gape even more. 'I just thought I'd check up on you. Given up, have we?'

'No! I'll figure it out. I'm…just taking a break, that's all.'

'Oh, did I not mention the time limit?'

I backed away from the mirrors, making room for others. Sam and Louis had moved on by now. I turned and faced Wilkes. 'No, you did not.'

'Tut, tut, tut…how remiss of me. Well, you have until midnight.'

'Tonight?'

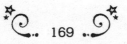

'Of course tonight,' said Wilkes. 'I can't hang around here forever, you know!'

'But–'

'Midnight. After that – *pfff*!' Wilkes raised his hands, wiggling his fingers to imitate dissolving into nothing.

'Hey, that's not fair!' I protested, but he was fading already. 'I won't stop nagging you, you know!' I yelled – but then he disappeared altogether. I turned around. Everyone else had stopped giggling at their reflections and they were staring at me in silence.

I waved. 'Yeah, hi! Er…it's a game, see. My brother and me, we…oh, never mind.' I bolted out.

Eternal Bloom

I had until midnight. Which was bad enough in itself, but then I was in for an even bigger shock.

I was excited when I saw that the car was back from the garage when we returned from the fair – and relieved to see the same junk still there. The inside hadn't been touched. But when I searched it, I couldn't find the key anywhere. I shoved my hand way down the back of the seat and everything, but it was no use. It just wasn't there.

I couldn't believe it.

So if it wasn't in the Hippo, and it wasn't in the car or the caves – I remembered checking my pocket just as I was leaving – then the only other place it could be was somewhere on the street between the Hellfire Caves and where Maro had picked me up. In which case, I didn't stand a chance of getting it back.

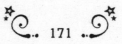

I dragged myself back indoors. Now what? 'Oh, Mr Wilkes, I seem to have mislaid that ancient key you gave me. Could you get another one cut, please?' Yeah, right. Meanwhile, the house still had that atmosphere hanging over it. I could almost taste it. I wondered if there had been any more weird night-time incidents. It was hard to tell – god knows, there'd been enough other catastrophes.

I went into the living room, where a duvet-wrapped Emily was watching TV with Flossie. Hetty was sprawled by the hearth.

Flossie jumped up. 'Kitty! How's, uh,' – she glanced at Emily – '*things?*'

'Oh, you know…'

'Come and watch,' said Em, patting the couch beside her.

'OK.' I flopped down. Ignoring the meaningful looks from Flossie, I tried to watch the movie. But nothing was sinking in, my head was elsewhere. Poor old Em kept coughing. She looked terrible…so pale she was practically transparent, and her breathing was bad…she was in lousy shape, basically. Which *really* didn't make me feel a whole lot better about the key situation. I tried to tell myself that Emily's illness was nothing to do with the curse, but a voice in my head kept saying *but what if it is?* And I'd had the key to this problem's solution in

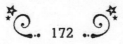

my hand, quite literally, and I'd lost it. What a complete moron.

What with all the torment over that, plus the bad atmosphere in the house, *I* was starting to feel pretty ill myself. I had to get out.

'Kitty?' said Floss, as I got up.

'Meh, I've seen this before…I think I'll take a walk. How about it, Hetty?'

Hetty did that doggy-raised-eyebrow thing that said 'who – me?', but it was the only part of her anatomy that moved.

'It's raining, Kitty,' said Flossie.

'Oh…yeah.' I looked out of the window. It was that fine, drenching drizzle that you know is planning to stick around for hours. Not that the boys seemed to care. They were out in the back garden, kicking a football around and obviously just loving that they were getting covered in mud. Idiots. Beyond them was the 'magic' ever-blooming rosebush, all brimming with white roses next to the barren sticks of its neighbours. Ha! Could it magic back that key for me? I wished.

Not knowing what else to do, I went for a wander. Hetty followed me into the dining room, which had become Charlie's temporary office. His work stuff was strewn all over the table. 'Oh, Het,' I sighed, as I gazed at

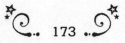

the portrait of Sir Ambrose. 'What am I going to do, eh?'

'*Wuffle*,' said Hetty.

'Yeah…'

The usual blank stare from Sir Ambrose.

'Oh, why can't you and Wilkes just…make up!' I said, knowing I was being completely ridiculous. One thing I knew about dead people – they didn't change their minds about *anything*.

I stared at the rose in his hand. He also had a white rose pattern on his waistcoat. What *was* it with all the white roses? I stared at the fancy frame with its three lions above and the motto below: 'Oh plant agen, eternal bloom', same as Emily had told me – only 'again' was spelled wrong, I noticed. Well, they did use some weird spellings back in those days.

Flossie appeared in the doorway. 'OK, I can't leave Em on her own for long, but…what's up? Is there a problem with–'

'Yes,' I said, and told her all about the lost key.

'Oh no!' said Flossie. 'What are you going to do?'

'Oh, it's cool – I'll just get the "magic rosebush" to bring it back for me. Bing! Just like in the movies. And everyone will live happily ever after.'

'You could try,' said Flossie.

'Flossie, I'm *kidding*.'

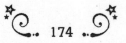

'I know, but…there *is* something special about it, isn't there? Otherwise it wouldn't bloom all year round. Maybe there's some spirit connected to it…'

'A Good Fairy, right.'

There was a vase full of the roses on the dining table. Flossie took one, waved it and chanted, 'The key shall be returned to yoooou! There – anything?'

It almost made me want to laugh…almost. ''Fraid not.'

The question 'What would Sam do?' filled my head. I *hated* to admit to myself that this was even worth asking, but hey, I was desperate. I eyed the open laptop on the table.

'Charlie's still out, right?' I said.

'Yes.'

I opened the browser on the laptop and did a search for 'white rose'.

'What are you doing?' asked Flossie.

I sighed. 'Channelling our swotty brother and arming myself with facts.'

I found a page about the 'White Rose of York'. I remembered the Wars of the Roses – one of the less boring things we'd learned about in school. But that was way earlier in history than Wilkes and Ambrose. 'Says here it was also the symbol of the Jacobites–'

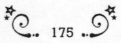

'The what-ites?'

'The Jacobites,' I said. 'They were upset when King James got chucked off the throne, and they fought over it…no, that's still too early. Nothing much else… OK, let's try Sir Ambrose.'

I skipped over the stuff about his early life, until the name John Wilkes cropped up. 'Check this out: "When Sir Ambrose's friend" – this Scottish guy, Bute – "came to head the government in 1762, Wilkes attacked them both in his publication, *The North Briton*, using an anti-Scots tone…" Oh, so that's why…'

'Why what?' said Flossie.

'Wilkes has – *had* – this *thing* about the Scots. Says here that Sir Ambrose was furious about the article, and did everything he could to see to it that Wilkes was arrested for it…Wilkes got sent to the Tower…'

Flossie gasped. 'Was he hanged?'

'No…says he was later released, but he never forgave Sir Ambrose.' I sighed and closed the browser. 'Well, this is all very well, but it's not going to help me find out if this vine-clad tomb really is the one where Sir Ambrose is buried, or get me inside it.'

'It's *got* to be,' said Flossie. 'I asked Emily about it. Apparently it does have ivy all over it. Hey, I just thought: maybe you could get into the tomb without a key.'

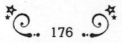

'What, break in?'

'Yeah. Or not even. Maybe it'll be all rusty and rotten and you can practically just walk in.'

I blinked at her. 'You know what, Floss? That's brilliant. Come on – let's give it a go. Oh wait, don't you have to go back to Emily?'

'She fell asleep,' said Flossie. 'Maro's here. She'll be fine. Hey, you know what else? Maybe the *tomb* is where you'll find Sir Ambrose's ghost.'

'I don't think… Oh, god.'

'What?' said Flossie.

'It's in a graveyard! The place'll be *teeming* with ghosts.' The images of Suki and Paul Whitehead loomed in my mind's eye. I felt ill again.

'Well, never mind…' said Flossie.

'No. Come on – let's do this!'

The Vine-Clad Tomb

As we entered the graveyard, I saw a handsome young soldier leaning against a tree, gazing at some ragged papers in his hand. World War Two, I reckoned. As we passed, I saw a tear roll down his dirty cheek. Then a disgusting figure came hobbling towards me – a man in a tricorn hat, with a face covered in revolting black growths. A pale little girl in Victorian dress and bare feet skipped among the graves. She was carrying what I thought was a doll, until I realized it was a dead baby.

'Ugh,' I said. 'It's all a bit grim. OK, let's see if we can find this tomb.'

'Emily says you can't miss it,' said Flossie. 'It's kind of big, and it's got an angel on it.'

We headed down a path until we came to a leafy corner of the graveyard.

'Maybe that's it,' said Flossie, as Hetty led the way to

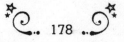

a large tomb with ivy growing over it. 'Hetty seems to think so.'

We drew closer. The tomb, topped with a mossy, crumbly angel, was large enough to be a one-room house for a very small person.

'Yup, look,' I said, pointing to the inscription:

SIR AMBROSE VYNER
1707–1769

Underneath was a bit of stuff about him, and next to that was a silhouette of him, carved in stone. At the far end were a couple of steps leading down to a wooden door. 'Well, so much for "rusty and rotten",' I said, as I pushed on it. 'It's solid as a rock.'

'Hmm…well, what about Sir Ambrose?' asked Flossie. 'Any sign of him?'

I looked around. 'Erm, no.'

'Maybe if you call him.'

'Don't be dumb…oh, all right. I'm that desperate. Sir Ambrose? Sir Ambrose!'

Nothing. Even the other St Mary's ghosts just drifted on by. 'I knew it…oh, this is stupid.'

Flossie was studying the inscription. 'What d'you suppose this means?'

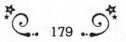

'What?'

'Look,' said Flossie. 'The last bit, after it says about him being an MP and everything…see?'

I read it. There it was again, the motto from the picture frame:

OH PLANT AGEN, ETERNAL BLOOM!

'It's to do with the white rose,' I said. 'Emily said – don't you remember? Oh no, you were busy with the karaoke. Well, they think it's a reference to that rosebush in the garden that blooms all the time. It doesn't help us. Come on, let's go.'

'No! Don't leave!' A strange metallic voice echoed from somewhere.

Hetty barked; Flossie squealed.

'Who's there?'

'It's meeee! Sir Aaaam-brose!'

I folded my arms. 'Right. Why don't you come out of there, Sam?'

The shrubbery next to the tomb rustled, and Darth Vader appeared – or rather Sam appeared, wearing some stupid Darth Vader helmety-thing. He pulled it off. 'Was I that unconvincing?'

'Yes.' I looked around. 'I hope Louis isn't with you?'

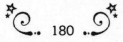

'No, he's on his way to Jonah's house. I'm going too. It's just that as we were leaving, I spotted you guys heading this way, and remembered you asking about Sir Ambrose's tomb earlier…I made an excuse so's I could follow you. Sorry, couldn't resist…'

'God, Sam. Anyway, I'm glad you're alone. But you're not to say anything to Louis about this, OK?'

'I won't.'

'Where'd you get that shirt?' asked Flossie. Sam had changed into an oversized England football shirt.

'Louis lent it to me. We got a bit muddy playing football in the rain.'

I rolled my eyes. 'Yeah, I saw. Maro's going to love you.' I stared at the shirt. Something struck me about it, but I couldn't quite figure out what it was. 'And by the way,' I added, 'as for your ghost impressions – the day you find a way to get *me* to hear you, but nobody else, you'll be a lot more convincing.'

'Yeah, well…how's it going, anyway? You think you're going to crack this?'

'Well, the trouble is, Kitty's lost–' Flossie began.

'*Time,*' I butted in, flashing her a look. 'Lost a bit of *time* this morning. But I'm getting there.'

'Come on, Kit, you can tell me,' said Sam. 'Where's this snuffbox?'

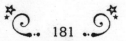

'I'll have it by tomorrow,' I said.

'But do you know where it is?'

'I told you, I'm *getting there*. In fact, I've made contact with the ghost of this John Wilkes guy, if you must know.'

Sam looked impressed. 'Cool! Ah, Kit, I've got to admit, I am a bit jealous. But no sign of old Sir Ambrose, eh?'

'Er…no. Don't know why. But then, I'm still amazed I got Wilkes. It helps to nag them, you know.'

'Maybe you just haven't nagged Sir Ambrose enough yet,' suggested Sam. He looked at his phone, which had sprung into life. 'Oh…Louis's ringing me. Better go.' He backed away, holding his thumbs up. 'Good luck!'

Five and a half hours left, and still no key. I checked the car again once we were back at the house, but of course the thing had not suddenly magically appeared. I'd nagged Sir Ambrose as hard as I could at the graveyard, but he wasn't talking. *Why?* I was running out of ideas…

I was in the kitchen drying off Hetty when Dinky came home from work. After looking in on Emily she came back down and flopped into a chair.

Hetty tried to pull away from me to greet her.

I tugged her back. 'Hetty, no! You're not dry yet!'

'Thanks for looking after her, Kitty,' sighed Dinky. 'And I see the car's all sorted. Thank you, Maro, you've been such a great help.' She pulled out her powder compact and grimaced at her reflection. Poor Dinky. Her eyes looked like they were sliding down her face, and I swear she might actually have lost weight from all the stress.

'It's nothing,' said Maro. 'I *would* have made us all dinner, but–'

'No, no, no, I told you, we're going out. My treat,' said Dinky, waving her compact about. 'Charlie's only too happy to stay here with Emily. There's a match he wants to watch on TV.'

'OK, well I made something just for them,' said Maro. She went to fill the kettle. 'Cup of tea?'

'Glass of *wine*, please,' said Dinky. Then she was foraging around in her bag while chit-chatting to Maro about whatever…I wasn't really listening, just working on Hetty with a head full of Wilkes and Sir Ambrose and the golden snuffbox, and then…

'…What's this?' said Dinky. 'Oh, it's that strange key.'

Key?! I looked up – Dinky was holding up *that* key, the one for Sir Ambrose's tomb. My heart skipped a beat. How the hell…?

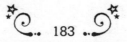

'Oh yes,' Maro was saying, as she poured out the glass of wine. 'Did you work out what it's for yet?'

Dinky stared at it. 'No idea.'

'Oh! Um, where was it?' I asked, trying to make it sound like a casual question.

'Dinky found it on the back seat of the car this morning,' said Maro. 'Hey, it's not yours, is it?'

'Nope.' I shrugged. What I wanted to do at this point was leap up, punch the air and go 'YAA-HOO!' but instead I just thrust all my energy into rubbing away at Hetty's coat. Thank god! The relief…

'Ah well,' said Dinky, dropping the key into a drawer. 'This goes in here, along with all the other mystery objects I'm always thinking I'll discover a use for one day. Right then, are we all ready to go out for dinner?'

At last! As everyone piled out of the house, I sneaked back into the kitchen, and got the key from the drawer. We were in business again.

That Devil Wilkes

At the old inn in the village, I kept checking my purse under the table to make sure the key was still there. I tried to eat, but was just too wound up inside.

Maro noticed. 'Are you all right, *pethaki-mou?*'

'Yeah, I'm fine,' I said. 'Just…not very hungry, that's all.' Dinky's family probably all thought I had an eating disorder by now. 'And…actually I have a headache. Do you mind if I go back to the house soon?'

'Oh, poor thing!' said Dinky. She reached into her handbag and pulled out some painkillers. 'Here, have a couple of these.'

'Thanks.' This was just as well actually, because what with all the stress and everything, I really did have a headache. But pretty soon I could say the medicine hadn't worked, make my excuses and leave while the others stuck around for dessert and coffee. Which,

judging by the way Dinky and Maro were chatting, would hopefully take a while.

I watched the clock; after fifteen minutes, I put my hand to my head and said, 'I'm sorry, but I'm still not feeling great. I think I just need to lie down.'

'Oh, sweetie!' said Maro. She put her napkin on the table and pushed back her chair. 'I'll walk you back.'

'No, no! It's only five minutes' walk. I'll be fine. Look, pudding's arrived.'

Sam jumped up. 'I'll go with you, Kit.' He winked at me – he could tell what this was really about.

As we left, I noticed Louis peering curiously after us.

'You can't come with me, you know,' I told Sam, once we were outside.

'I know,' said Sam. 'Just…good luck, eh? And be careful. Here, I've got something for you.' He reached into his pocket and pulled out a torch.

I took it from him. 'Thanks, Sam.'

'That doesn't count as help from a boy, OK?'

'OK.'

'But next time I'm coming with you, all right?'

'All right.'

'Well, see ya.' He patted me on the back, and went back inside. I was alone.

It was nearly nine o'clock. All the rainclouds had

gone, and the sky glittered with stars. My head was nice and clear now, too. I wrapped my jacket tightly around me and headed off to St Mary's churchyard.

Man, it was quiet around here. Way different from how it was back in my old neighbourhood in London. The place would be teeming with people, all going out to bars and restaurants... But here...once you got about five inches away from the steamy hum of the old inn, you were blanketed in a still, dark nothing. As I got closer to the churchyard, the only signs of life were... well not actual life at all, just ex-life. And wow, it was crowded tonight. The soldier, the girl, the guy with the disfigured face...they were all here, and loads more. None of them looked like Sir Ambrose, though. Clutching the key in my pocket, I ignored the ghosts as best I could, and headed over to his tomb.

It was so dark around this part, I could hardly see a thing. I took out the torch Sam had given me and shone it around. The beam fell on the mossy angel looming over me, and on the inscription, 'O plant agen, eternal bloom!' Finally, I went down the stone steps to the little door. *Oh, please let this be the right tomb!* I suddenly thought, as I rattled the key around in the lock. I was aware of movement behind me...or was it just the wind rustling in the trees? Right now I didn't

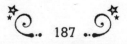

know whether I'd rather be out here, or inside the Vyner tomb.

I jiggled the key some more and at last I felt something turning. There was a click. I pushed. The creaking of the door echoed around the stone chamber. Not daring to think for a moment about what I might find in there, I stepped inside.

'Hello?'

Hello, hello-o-o-o…

Something scuttled past my feet. My torch shone on a dark shape…a rat. I shuddered.

'W-Wilkes?'

Ilkes, ilkes…

It felt weird speaking out loud in that cold, saturating darkness, what with the echo and everything. I shone the torch around the tomb. There were clusters of old vases and remnants of candles, and here and there were crumbly statues and busts of Roman gods or whatever, kind of like in the caves. And on the back wall there was a recess with a very dusty old urn inside it. I noticed white roses painted on it…more white roses…

'Sir Ambrose?'

Brose, brose…

Well, so much for nagging him. There was a gust of wind outside, and now on the back of it came a tune…like someone was humming to themselves. It sounded like the national anthem. The thought of there being anyone else in the graveyard at this time of night, let alone some patriotic nutter, filled me with dread. What if they found me here? I didn't dare shut the door, because the creaking would only attract attention.

The humming drew nearer – and yet I couldn't hear any footsteps. Perhaps it was not a live person after all, but a ghost – perhaps it was Sir Ambrose! I stood with my back to the wall beside the door. Now the humming turned to full-on singing…it was a man's voice, and he was singing the wrong words. As they grew louder and clearer instead of 'God save the Queen', there were the words 'victory bring!' I thought I recognised the voice, but needed to hear more…now he was really belting it out:

'May he sed-i-tion hush, and like a torrent rush, re-bell-ious *Scots* to crush, Goh-od save the King!'

Wilkes.

I stepped forward, and there he stood in the doorway, looking as if he was lit from within – I didn't need a torch beam to see him. He carried a cane. Tucking it under his arm, he ended the song with a salute and a heavy-jawed grin.

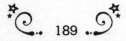

'May I come in?' he said, stepping in anyway.

'What was that all about?' I asked.

'The song? Well, if you'd ever bothered to find out what Sir Ambrose did to upset me so much, you wouldn't need to ask,' said Wilkes.

'Nothing he did could possibly justify what *you* did to *him*,' I snapped. 'Now, where's that snuffbox?'

'Ah, but this is part of the *deal*,' said Wilkes. 'You summoned me! Yet you show no interest in my side of the story. One's feelings can be hurt, you know.'

I was really angry now. 'Part of the deal?' I groaned. 'Fine. Go on, tell me! But I'm telling you now, you won't get a *milligram* of sympathy from me.'

'Tut tut, temper, temper! *So* like a Scot.'

'I'm not–'

'...Not Scottish, no!' interrupted Wilkes. He roared with laughter, showing all his crooked yellow teeth. 'And who can blame you for dissociating yourself from that coarse race of heathens?'

'No, I'm not – *they're* not!' I snapped. 'What the hell have you got against them, anyway?'

Wilkes waved his cane furiously. 'They tried to take over the throne, of course! Wretched Jacobites!'

Jacobites...the white roses...

'Your beloved Sir Ambrose was one of them,' Wilkes

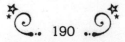

ranted on. "'O plant agen, eternal bloom!" His idea of wit, you know. "Plantagenet" – get it? Plant again *on the throne* a Stuart–'

'King James?' I said.

'Yes, and then later his grandson Charles...oh, they kept *on* about it. Anyway, the Stuarts were descended from the Plantagenets, you see? Wars of the Roses and all that. Well, they failed both times with the monarchy, so then what did they do? Tried to sneak one in to run the government, didn't they. Bute – another damned Stuart!'

'Well, why shouldn't a Scot run the country? It's a united kingdom! Anyway, I know all about you being sent to the Tower and everything...'

'Ah, not completely ignorant then,' said Wilkes.

'No, amazingly enough, even though I'm a mere *female*.'

Wilkes was fierce now. 'The king was wrong to do that, and the people knew it! *Crowds* of them, there were – outside the Tower, crying "Liberty! Liberty! Wilkes forever!" ' He shook his fist in the air.

I folded my arms. 'I. Don't. Care!' I said, through gritted teeth. 'If you think you're going to change my mind about this, you've got another thing coming. Now show me where that snuffbox is.'

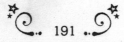

He didn't answer. Instead, he glanced down, and said, 'No use trying to bribe me, you know. I have no use for money.'

'*Huh?*'

He pointed with the cane. 'There. In your pocket.'

The crumpled page from Dinky's book was poking out of my pocket. I'd forgotten it was there. 'It's not a bribe, for god's sake. It's a picture of you,' I said, pulling it out and showing it to him. 'A clue that led me to track you down in the caves.'

Wilkes looked at it. His lip curled. 'Ah, yes...the murderous pencil.' He paused, then added, 'I think the artist rather regretted drawing that wicked portrait. He died, you know, not long after.' And he smirked at me, as if to say, *and that was no coincidence.*

It sent a shockwave through me, a grim reminder. I realised I'd got so wrapped up in solving the mystery, I'd almost forgotten I was dealing with someone who was *dangerous.* Could he have the power to do more harm, even from beyond the grave...to me? What the hell was I doing here? I had to be out of my tiny mind.

'Aha! That's more like it,' said Wilkes, stepping forward. 'At last...you're afraid!'

I stepped back. 'N-no I'm not.' Yeah, really convincing.

'And so you should be. You don't know who you're dealing with.'

'Of c-course I do.'

'That's a better portrait of me, there,' said Wilkes, striding over and indicating one of the Roman-y type busts with his cane. He chuckled. 'My last gift to Sir Ambrose, ha ha ha! Generous of me, don't you think?'

I shone my torch on the bust. 'That's not you...it looks nothing like you.'

Wilkes smirked. 'I have many guises.'

I was more confused than ever. Even weirder, there was a strange inscription at the base of the bust that was definitely not Latin:

נ ר ו ן ק ס ר

'The letters are Aramaic,' explained Wilkes. 'And they reveal my true identity. Only when you know that, will I grant you your wish...at a price, as ever.'

'But you said this was the last test, you–'

'You have some paper. Do you have something to write with?'

I fumbled in my bag and found the pen I'd used for the last riddle. My hands wouldn't stop shaking now. I was actually starting to feel ill, and just wanted to get

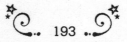

out of there. But I couldn't give up now. I had to lift the curse. Whatever it took.

'The Aramaic letters translate as N, R, O, N,' said Wilkes. 'Then Q, S, R.'

I wrote the letters on the back of the Wilkes picture, leaning on the wall while clumsily gripping the torch with my other hand.

'It means "Nero Caesar",' said Wilkes.

My God, I thought. *He is actually crazy.* I was dealing with a lunatic who thought he was a Roman emperor and was just going to keep giving me the run-around forever. He started on with some nonsense about each letter having a 'numerical value', but I wasn't having any more of this. I stuffed the pen, paper and torch into my bag. 'Forget it,' I said. 'I'm out of here.'

'As you wish!' said Wilkes.

I headed for the door, but just as I reached it, it slammed shut.

'No!' I grabbed the iron handle, but it came away in my hand. I fell back and *whack*, hit the cold, hard stone floor. Now the blackness was all around me. The glowing Wilkes had disappeared and there wasn't a glimmer of light anywhere. I felt in my bag for the torch, but I hadn't zipped up the bag…the torch must have fallen out. I felt around for it on the dirt floor, panic rising in my throat.

Yes! Here it was. I switched it on. It flickered yellow for a few seconds, then went out. How come? The batteries hadn't fallen out. I bashed it, but it was no use – the thing was dead. I stumbled over to the door and blindly felt on the floor for the detached handle. Then I remembered my phone. To hell with not getting help from boys, I needed Sam. I took it out, once again pathetically grateful for that tiny glowing screen. But then my heart sank again – no signal.

'The numerical value reveals my identity!' came Wilkes's disembodied voice. 'Now, "N" equals fifty. And there are two of them. Which makes…?'

'A hundred…look, let me out, *please.*'

'Two "R"s as well. Two times two hundred?'

Now I felt like crying. 'Four hundred,' I whimpered.

'…Which adds up to five hundred. Then "O" is six, "Q" is a hundred, and "S" is sixty. Which makes…what?'

'Six…a hundred…A hundred and sixty-six. Added to five hundred is…um…'

I knew, of course. But my voice had just completely dried up.

Six hundred and sixty-six. 666. The mark of the Beast…the Devil.

Lions

The logical part of my brain still told me I was dealing with a nutter – not that there was anything particularly reassuring about that.

But shut inside that tomb, unable to see anything or to get out, I was numb with fear now. What if I really had summoned the devil? It didn't matter how many times I reminded myself that I hadn't actually believed those stories of devil-worship…here in this dark, dark place, I was having dark, dark thoughts. The feeling of sheer, cold terror enveloped me now.

I heard his laughter echoing all around, cruel and mocking. Tiny shuffling noises told me the rats were back. And now there was the stench of sulphur again…

I got up and hammered my fists on the door. 'Help!' I yelled, but what use was that? Who would hear?

Maybe some of the graveyard ghosts would – maybe not. But what use were they, anyway?

Bang, bang, bang. 'Help!' I went on calling, not knowing what else to do. I gagged on the foul, stinking air.

'*Ha ha ha ha ha!*' went the laughter.

But this is a churchyard, for heaven's sake! I thought. Hallowed ground. Shouldn't I be protected from evil forces here?

Desperate, I hooked my finger into the hole left by the missing handle and pulled. The door was heavy and seemed wedged into place by some unseen force. I pulled harder, my finger straining…and the door gave just a tiny bit, enough for me to wedge my other hand into the gap. Now I had some leverage. I grunted as I tugged…now my arm was through…now my shoulder…

'Euuurgh!' I was out.

I scrambled up the steps, and there was Wilkes, right in front of me.

'Only joking!' he chuckled.

'Get away from me!' I yelled. I ran down the cemetery path, dodging the wandering ghosts.

Once again, Wilkes materialised in front of me. 'Tut-tut-tut,' he said. 'Can't take a joke, can we? Just like old Sandwich…'

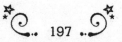

I whizzed past, determined not to be taken in by anything he said. *That's what the Devil always does in stories*, I thought. *He tricks people.*

I reached the gate. Gasping for breath now, I lifted the latch and bolted out, almost colliding with Sam.

'Sam!' I was quite hysterically happy to see him.

'God, you've been ages,' he said. 'Are you all right?'

'I…oh, I just want to get out of here!'

'Come on, I'll walk with you to Dinky's,' said Sam, and we started along the deserted village high street. 'We'd better hurry up, though. They're about to leave the restaurant. What happened?'

'He…I…oh, it's too awful!' I said. 'I feel sick.'

'OK, well you're safe now,' said Sam.

Suddenly Wilkes appeared right in front of me again. 'Have you no sense of fun? It was a *joke*, I tell you!'

'Go away!' I snapped. 'You can't hurt me now!'

'Er…what?' said Sam, who of course couldn't see him.

'He's the Devil, and he won't leave me alone!'

'The Devil? Er, what does he look like?'

'He's in the *guise* of John Wilkes, but–'

'Kitty, don't be–'

'Yes, I know it sounds nuts, but trust me, there was this awful smell like those stink bombs – brimstone, you know – and he sh-showed me…he showed me this inscription, and it was code for the Mark of the Beast, and–'

'Kitty, Kitty,' interrupted Sam. 'Listen to yourself! Have you forgotten the baboon trick in the caves?'

'You tell her,' said Wilkes, now appearing on the bonnet of a nearby parked car. 'She won't listen to me.'

The baboon trick. Poor old Lord Sandwich, thinking he was confronted with the Devil. Oh god! Had I really fallen for another version of the same gag? 'But this was different, Sam! There was…it was…' I trailed off. Now that I thought about it, it wasn't so different at all. And I remembered what Wilkes said when he first appeared to me: *'We could have some fun here.'*

'If that's your idea of a joke,' I growled at Wilkes, 'it's not funny!'

He jumped down and stood before me. 'Young lady, I apologise for that tasteless prank,' he said, giving a deep bow, like I was a princess or something. 'It was most ungallant of me. Please forgive me. You really have been quite clever and brave…for a female. So now, if you want to know where the…'

The rest of his sentence was drowned out by Sam who couldn't hear any of this and said, 'Kitty, you've got to–'

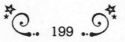

I put my hand over his mouth. 'Shush! What did you say?'

'I shhd yuve gt to–' Sam tried.

'Not you – him! Wilkes, what did you say?'

He spread his arms like a hammy actor, and delivered his final riddle:

'Now we have come to the end of the game!
I'll ne'er return, but here's the story:
Heraldic beasts are all in the frame;
Three of them form his crowning glory! Goodbye.'

And with one last cross-eyed grin, he was gone.

I stood there, staring. My hand fell away from Sam's mouth. 'Heraldic beasts…all in the frame…three of them,' I muttered.

'What?' said Sam.

'Never mind. I can't ask your help, you're a boy…oh, but this is so close, I can taste it!'

We'd just gone past the old inn. The door opened, spilling the hum of voices into the night, and the others came out. 'Kitty…Sam!' said Maro. 'What are you doing out here?'

'Oh…we were just chatting. I'm feeling much better now!' I probably seemed quite hysterical, and no doubt

the grin I gave her was more church gargoyle than anything remotely reassuring. I thrust my arm around Flossie and marched ahead with her.

'Floss, help me out,' I hissed. 'I've had my final clue: "Heraldic beasts are all in the frame: three of them form his crowning glory." What do you think?'

'Crowning glory?' said Flossie. 'What is it – a crown? A hat? Is this about that red cap again?'

'No, no, I don't think so…heraldic beasts…all in the frame…'

'What frame?' said Flossie.

I stared at her. 'The frame…'

I stared back at Sam.

I stared at the logo on the England shirt he was still wearing. 'Heraldic beasts…three of them…'

Bing! Finally, it all clicked into place. I remembered where I'd recently seen something very similar. 'That's it!' I said. I turned to face the others, wide-eyed. 'Lions!'

They gaped at me, then looked at each other.

'Kitty?' said Maro. 'Are you OK, *pethaki-mou?*'

'Yes, I'm fine…it's just that I need to…' I couldn't even get the words out. It all fitted. I knew at last where the snuffbox was…there was no doubt in my mind. I turned and ran all the way back to Dinky's.

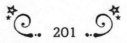

'Kitty!' said Charlie, as he opened the front door. 'Is anything the matter?'

'The curse!' I blurted. 'I know all about it…and I'm going to put a stop to it, right now!' Dodging Hetty as she lumbered up to greet me, I hurtled into the dining room.

Charlie followed. As I dragged a chair over to the portrait of Sir Ambrose, stood on it and grabbed the portrait, he called out, 'Hang on, just a minute!'

Hetty wasn't happy either. She started barking, though she couldn't seem to figure out whose side to be on.

'Don't worry,' I yelled, as I lifted the painting off its hook and brought it to the table. 'It'll be fine, trust me!'

Woof, woof!

'H-how do you know about the… Kitty, I must insist that you – aah!'

Having rushed to my side, Charlie lurched back as I pulled a knife out of the sideboard and turned towards the painting with it. I hadn't meant to wave it in his direction, but that's kind of what happened.

He recovered and reached for my wrist as I went for the ornate gilt frame with the knife…but then Hetty was in the way and he stumbled as he tried to step over her.

Three heraldic lions, right there in the frame above

Sir Ambrose's head. *The crowning glory...* Just as the others arrived, I plunged the knife into the back of the oval shape at the top of the frame.

'Kitty! What on earth are you doing?' demanded Dinky.

The gilded plaster fell away easily. I reached in and pulled out a small gold box. 'Here it is!'

Everyone looked amazed, including Emily, who had come downstairs to see what all the fuss was about. Most brilliantly, *Louis* looked amazed.

Only Hetty was still in a state of hyped-up confusion. '*Woof*,' she said. '*Woof?*'

I'd done it.

Settling a Score

'Oh my…' Dinky gasped.

'Bloody hell!' said Louis.

I just stood there and stared at the little golden box in my hand, still not quite believing it myself. I'd done it! I'd actually solved the riddles. I'd actually found the *thing*.

'Although, you know, this doesn't actually prove–' began Louis, but he didn't finish, because then something even more incredible happened.

There was a sort of…shuddering. Like a small earthquake. Candlesticks rumbled across the table. Lamps wobbled. Em ran to her mum, Hetty got all het up again…Maro said a bunch of things in Greek.

Then it stopped.

Faint shapes appeared, floating midair, like pale skins being pushed about. There was that bonfire smell again,

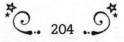

like I'd smelled the night the books flew out of the dresser.

Then a horrible figure emerged. Half the flesh of its face was missing, so that the nose was no more than a stub, the left eye bulged like it was about to fall out, and the teeth showed where they shouldn't, giving it a ghastly lopsided grin. Scraps of white hair hung in random clumps around oozing patches of pink scalp, and the whole figure looked blackened and charred, with rags for clothes.

'Argh!' I cried.

I knew right away that I was the only one who could see this. Everyone else was behaving as if it wasn't there, and the adults were bombarding me with questions, questions…I knew I had to get them out. I mean, not that I *wanted* to be alone with this grotesque spirit, or demon, or whatever it was…but I would have to be strong.

Thank god for Sam, who seemed to understand what was going on. He signalled to Maro, and the two of them got everyone out.

I was alone with…it.

He – at least it might have been a he – stood there, gazing at the snuffbox. Then he tried to speak, but his words sounded slurred and weighed down:

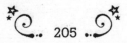

'I nng…been nng…shearching…for so nng… long…'

He reached out. His hand swiped at the snuffbox, his fingers lit up and the light travelled up his arm, then through the whole of him, until all the burned rags were transformed into fine clothes. The burned smell disappeared and his flesh was restored… Suddenly I could see that this was no demon but a gentleman, as smart and well-groomed as in his portrait.

'Sir Ambrose!' I gasped.

His eyes had been closed during the transformation. Now he opened them and gazed up at the ceiling. 'It's almost time for me to go.' The voice was normal now. He turned to me. 'You…you were here before.'

'Yes…yes, I was. And you were trying to communicate with me, weren't you? You showed me the picture.'

'Now *that*,' said Ambrose, 'that was hard. *Lord knows*, it was hard. And there was damage, I fear…'

I shrugged. 'Oh well, you know…what can you do, eh? Um, I guess that was you with the red sock, as well, right?'

'Ah, the Phrygian Cap – yes.' He pronounced it 'fridge-ee-an'. 'One has to be resourceful in such circumstances.'

'That *was* a bit brilliant,' I said. 'If a bit freaky at the time.'

'"Freaky"?'

'Yeah, I mean…never mind. I never did find out where that, um, *Phrygia* place was, though.'

'Ancient Anatolia,' said Ambrose. 'Asia Minor. The hat is a symbol of liberty, something of which Mister… *Wilkes*' – he practically hissed the name – 'seems to consider himself a great exponent. But liberty for whom, may I ask? Liberty for *whom*?' He was puffing himself up into a rage, which was clearly too much for his fragile spirit. 'Aah…ooohh,' he wailed, and he started to fade.

'OK…you can rest in peace now,' I said. 'No more demons holding you back.'

His image grew stronger again. 'Demons?'

'You know…the demons or whatever you want to call them – evil spirits. The ones that were sent by the curse.'

'Curse? That nonsense? Good heavens, no! Wilkes is all bluster and perfidious trifle, no more capable of putting a curse on someone than I am…I mean, was. This was about settling an old score, d'you see? As long as he had that snuffbox hidden away, he'd WON.'

I could hardly believe it. That was *it*? A stupid bit of point-scoring over a bit of fake black magic? *That* was

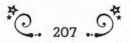

what had caused all the glass-smashing and the book-throwing? Jeez. Did boys *never* actually grow up?

'But...isn't it true that things didn't exactly, um, go well for you after that?' I asked. 'How do you know it wasn't down to the curse?'

'Ah, the seeds were sown long before, alas. My marriage was a sham...I had a hereditary condition... there *was no curse.*'

'But the fire,' I said. 'Wasn't *that* caused by the curse?'

He shook his head. 'No...no.'

I didn't like to say it, but I was thinking, *how can you be so sure of that?* A whole bunch of other questions were forming in my head, but there was no time to ask them. He was fading.

'I must go,' he said. 'Thank you...'

Then he was gone...and I knew he was gone for good.

I walked into the living room, carrying the little golden box. Everyone stopped talking and looked at me.

Maro got up and flung her arms around me. '*Kitaki-mou!* Are you OK?'

'Um, yeah.'

They all gazed at me expectantly.

'You won't have any more trouble,' I said.

'Maro has told us about your phantorama, Kitty,' said Dinky. 'I can hardly believe it! You are a very special girl!'

I looked over at Emily, who was sitting on the couch. So if her illness was nothing to do with the 'curse', would she get better now or not?

'Em knows all about it,' said Sam, reading my mind.

'Oh…really?' I knew the family had kept Emily in the dark about the 'curse', as they hadn't wanted to scare her.

Emily beamed at me. 'Yeah, you're amazing, Kitty!'

'Oh, well…' I bit my lip. Now this was tricky… should I let them go on believing they'd been under some terrible curse, or should I tell them what Sir Ambrose had just explained to me?

In the time it took me to step forward and put the snuffbox down on the coffee table, I'd made up my mind. I would have to let them think I'd lifted the curse. Not to make myself seem more important or anything… god, no! I was well embarrassed. Wasn't thrilled that they knew about my phantorama at all. All I'd wanted was to fix everything quietly and let them think – well all right, let everyone except *Louis* – think that I'd found the snuffbox by chance.

No. I was thinking of Emily. It was better for her this

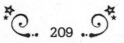

way, because if she believed that the only reason she'd fallen ill in the first place was because of a curse that was now gone…well, it followed that she would believe she was all cured now. And believing that, I reckoned, would help her to get better for real.

'Right, this calls for a celebration!' announced Dinky, getting up. She went and got a bunch of goodies from the kitchen – cookies, brownies, ice cream…and wine.

I suddenly noticed I was famished. I piled a dish full of ice cream and brownies. Next thing we knew, Dinky was insisting we stay the night, inviting the neighbours over to join the celebration. She was in total OTT excitement mode.

I scoffed my dessert, then left the adults to it and disappeared upstairs.

I was about to follow the girls into Emily's room, when Louis caught my arm. 'Hey, Kitty! I just wanted to say…thank you!'

'Er, thanks. I mean, that's OK.'

'It was really incredible,' said Louis. 'Respect! To be honest, I did think you kind of had a screw loose.'

'Well, I showed you then, didn't I?'

Louis winced.

Sam, coming up the stairs behind us, laughed. 'You asked for that one, Louis.'

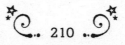

'Well, of course this means you're now a member of the Ins—'

'…Insula Club,' I said, finishing his sentence for him. 'Yeah, thanks but no thanks. I just wanted to show you and your mates what a mere *girl* could do.'

'Hey, I never said—'

'You didn't need to, Louis.' And again I made for Emily's door.

'Wait,' said Louis, pulling me back again.

I sighed. '*What?*'

'I'm sorry.'

'Huh?'

'You know, me and my mates, we wind each other up all the time – man, we are *brutal.* It's just our way. So…I guess what I'm saying is, don't think you were singled out for that treatment, because you weren't.'

'Gee, thanks.'

'Ah, don't be like that! I mean…oh, who cares, it's just dumb macho rubbish. Not *real* brave stuff like you do, with all the ghosts and everything.'

'Yup, well, anyway, you guys are going to France, and we're off to the West Country tomorrow…'

'Yeah, I know,' said Louis. 'I wish—'

'…So being a member of your club isn't exactly going to mean anything, is it?'

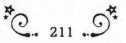

'Hey, it's a badge of honour!'

'Don't flatter yourself,' I said, punching him gently on the arm. In spite of myself, I couldn't help smiling slightly. 'Anyway, what do you wish?'

Louis looked away. 'Oh, nothing. Just...like I say, what you did was awesome. We've all been so worried about Em.'

And then there was that misty look in those wide-set alien eyes of his, like I glimpsed that time before we went to the fair. It made something go all squirmy inside my belly.

My voice softened. 'She's already better, Louis. Just listen.'

Coming out of Emily's room was the most ear-splitting noise – Emily was singing karaoke.

The Secret

'Kitty?'

I opened one eye. It was Dinky. 'Mm, hi,' I mumbled.

Dinky bounced in wearing her dressing gown. 'Oh, Kitty, what a wonderful night! Not a single disturbance! Oh, I feel so *alive*, so *awake*…haven't slept like that in ages!'

I rolled over on the couch. 'What timezit?'

'Seven,' said Dinky. 'Want some tea?'

Seven? I hadn't got to bed until one! 'Er, no… thangzzz.'

'Oh, poor baby. I'm sorry! You sleep. I just wanted to let you know how happy I am!'

And she bounced out again, singing to herself.

I didn't wake again until nine-thirty, by which time the whole household was in a state of chaos, getting ready to go to France first thing the next morning.

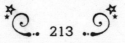

Which they were all extra-specially excited about, since they'd nearly had to cancel the trip.

I found Maro in the dining room, clearing away the breakfast things. I gave her a hand. 'So,' I said. 'It's all systems go, is it?'

'Yes,' said Maro, as she stacked the dishes on the breakfast trolley. 'They do still have to take Emily to the doctor, to check she's well enough to travel, but she'll be able to get as much rest as she needs there, so they don't expect there to be any problems. Oh, and guess what we found out last night.'

'What?'

'Apparently the people who lived here before had problems, too – and the ones before them, *and* the ones before them.'

'Really?'

'Mm-hm. The neighbours eventually let it slip. But of course the sellers never said anything about it to Dinky and Charlie, because they were desperate to move out.'

'What? That's terrible!'

'Yes,' said Maro. 'But be honest now: if *you* were living in a house that was cursed, and there was nothing you could do to stop it, what would you do?'

'Um…well, I'd… Hmm.'

'Exactly,' said Maro. 'Who wants to live their whole

life like that? Pure hell! Hardly surprising. Anyway, of course the neighbours were *dying* to know what had been going on.'

'Oh no, I hope—'

'Don't worry, we didn't let on about anything, not the smashed glasses – none of it. The neighbours were surprised, but relieved as well. They were fed up of having new people coming in, then freaking out and putting the place on the market when they couldn't stand it any longer. They didn't much like the house standing here all boarded up for ages, either. Anyway, it cleared up one thing.'

'What's that?'

'Emily's illness,' said Maro. 'It's unlikely to have anything to do with the curse. We asked. None of those people that lived here before got any serious illnesses. No bad accidents, either.'

'Actually, I know why that is.' I explained all about my encounter with the ghost of Sir Ambrose, and how the whole curse thing was just a great big joke. 'Emily just got ill, that's all. Like people do. Same with Charlie's fall. It's a coincidence.'

'Oh, *that* was no coincidence!' said Maro. 'He was stressed and sleep-deprived, poor guy.'

'True. Look, you might as well tell Dinky. But I still

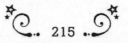

think they shouldn't tell Emily – not until she's over this. I think believing the curse is lifted is helping her get better.'

'Oh!' said Maro. 'You are so right. But I will tell Dinky. *Thank you*, Kitty!' She took my head in her hands and planted a great big smacker on my forehead. 'And your efforts were not wasted – you've rid this house of its poltergeist! You are a brave, clever girl.'

GHOST BLOG

SUNDAY 10 APRIL 3.00PM

We've just stopped over at the Hellfire Caves again. They're not exactly on the way to where we're going, but I bugged Maro about it and she didn't mind, after all I did for Dinky and her family.

I gave Carol a drawing I'd done of the Sukie ghost – minus the gory bits. 'That's how I imagine her,' I lied. Carol thanked me, and said she hoped I'd enjoyed doing my project. I said yeah, well, it's been pretty hard work, then Maro goes, 'It's a HUGE success!' which made me turn beetroot.

As we left, I gazed back at the place and thought of poor old Sukie and Paul Whitehead, stuck there forever,

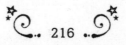

both searching for things they'll never find.

I felt REALLY sorry for them.

Maro asked me what was up, so I told her I wished I could help the other Hellfire ghosts.

She said I'd drive myself crazy if I went on thinking like that.

And then Sam said the people that run the Caves wouldn't WANT to get rid of their ghosts anyway, 'cause they're part of the attraction. Which, OK, I guess he has a point...but at the time it SO bugged me, because just how spectacularly missing-the-point can you get? It's all about relieving the PAIN and ANGUISH, stupid. But hey, he's a boy, what do you expect.

Anyway, Maro's right. If I CAN fix something, I will. And actually, despite all the horror, it feels FANTASTIC to be able to do that. Like having a superpower! Only I didn't save Emily's life, as it turns out...OK, I'm not THAT much of a superhero.

Ha! Just as I was writing that, Maro got a text saying Emily's definitely on the mend. Well, that's good to know. Just 'cause her illness was nothing to do with the 'curse', doesn't mean it couldn't still have dragged on and got worse.

I've been wondering about Wilkes. Did I release him too, like I did Sir Ambrose? No. Thinking about it, that

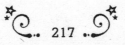

217

doesn't seem right. No way was he a tormented spirit! He wasn't trawling the mortal world, endlessly worrying that he might have caused trouble with the whole 'curse' business. Which leads to the question, what the heck WAS he doing here, then?

HMM…

OK, here's my theory:

SOME SPIRITS JUST HANG OUT IN THE MORTAL WORLD FOR THE HELL OF IT.

Maybe they have no choice, maybe they do. How do I know? But they stick around, even though they don't have any 'unfinished business'. Which would explain how I was able to 'summon' Wilkes the way I did, plus how expert he was at showing up in different places, making a stink, slamming doors…he'd had loads of practice. So even though he told me he wasn't ever coming back, I reckon that just meant he wasn't coming back FOR ME. He's going to mess with other people's heads.

Yup – he's ready and waiting. The devil.

Glossary of Maro-isms

Pethaki-mou [pe-**tha**-ki moo]......my little child

Agapi-mou [a-**gah**-pee moo]......my love

Kitaki-mou [Kit-**ak**-i moo]......my little Kitty

Endaksi [en-**dak**-si]......OK

Kalimera [kali-**mare**-ah]......hello

The-eh mou! [the-**eh** moo]......my god!

Pethakia [pe-**tha**-ki-ah]......children

Kamari-mou [ka-**mar**-i moo]......my pride and joy

Ti einai? [tee **ee**-neh]......what is it?

Acknowledgements

Many thanks to Vicky at the Hellfire Caves, for all her help.

Any resemblance to a particular dead person is entirely intentional. However, I have used my Artistic Licence, of which I am sure he would approve. For information on the real John Wilkes, see http://en.wikipedia.org/wiki/John_Wilkes. Here you will also find the drawing of Wilkes that is ripped from the history book; it is by William Hogarth.

Questions and Answers with Fiona Dunbar

Where did the idea for the *Kitty Slade* books come from?

My starting point was actually a desire to write a series about kids solving mysteries, along the lines of Enid Blyton's *Famous Five* series, only updated. Then I revisited a story I started way back in 2004 called *Kit & Nan*, about a boy and his grandmother touring the country as a kind of ghostbusting team, and I really wanted to use that concept in some way. So Kit became Kitty, the grandmother got put into the background as Maro, and a brother and sister were added in. And of course Kitty isn't providing a professional service; any ghostbusting that occurs is purely incidental. The other source of inspiration was places I'd been to on holiday: everywhere I went, I'd go, 'This place is amazing: I really want to write a story set here!'

How did you come up with the title *Fire and Roses*?

That was easy: the subject matter was a gift, as will become clear to anyone who reads it. In fact I did want to call it *Hellfire & Roses*, because of the references to the Hellfire Club, but it was felt that the word 'hell' might be a bit misleading as to the content of the book. No, Kitty does not literally descend into the inferno! Roses play a prominent symbolic part.

Kitty can see ghosts - do you believe in ghosts and have you ever seen one?

Oh, did I not mention that these books are autobiographical? OK, I'm kidding. No, disappointingly, I've never seen a ghost. I'm still hoping. But my mum visited me in spirit once – albeit invisibly – a couple of days after she died. So I do feel that's evidence that an energy force can linger on for a while after somebody is gone.

One of your earlier series (the *Lulu Baker* trilogy) was made into a BBC TV series called *Jinx*. How did it feel to see your characters on television?

It was brilliant! I got to meet Lulu, Frenchy and 'Minty' – AKA Varaminta. I thought they were all fabulous. Only Minty was far too nice – in the books, of course, she is monstrous. But there are different rules for a TV sitcom: because there is no major story arc, characters have to be the same in every show. It simply wouldn't have worked for her to be evil: you are limited to 'slightly annoying'.

What's next for Kitty Slade?

Venus Rocks! Kitty encounters a ghost ship in Cornwall. Things get seriously weird under the sea...

Follow Fiona Dunbar
www.fionadunbar.com

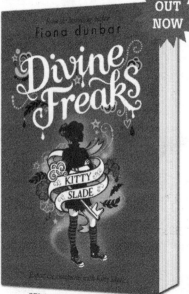